ECO WORRIER

Ian Slatter

Illustrated by Paul Winward

ianslatter.com
@slatter_ian
paulwinwardillustration.com

Free download offer

Join my Readers Club and receive a **free short story**, plus updates about new books (including sneak peeks) and special offers.

Visit ianslatter.com for further details.

The characters and events portrayed in this book are fictitious. Any similarity to real persons, living or dead, is coincidental and not intended by the author.

ECO WORRIER

First edition. June 23, 2020.

Written by Ian Slatter.

ISBN: 9798648205529

I hate politics

'So anyway,' Marty continued, 'after that a pair of velociraptors wandered out of the toilets and into our classroom, licking their lips and burping because they'd just eaten Jamie Tancock, who'd just gone in for his one o-clock poo, but luckily we were saved by some aliens who all looked just like The Queen, who'd just landed on the cricket pitch, who kindly blew them up with their laser cannons. Of course, then we were all abducted and subjected to hours of torture on their spaceship, but they returned us all in time for home time.'

'Oh, that's good then,' said his mum, without her eyes leaving the TV.

Marty sighed. No-one ever listened to a word he said. He was getting used to it now. When the Politics Channel was on at tea-time he really couldn't expect to get any sort of conversation out of either his mum or Emily, his little sister. His mum had an excuse he supposed, what with being the Prime Minister and all that, but Emily? What was her problem? She was an eleven-year-old girl. Why was she so interested in politics?

Everyone said she looked and sounded just like her mum, which she seemed to love. Fortunately, nobody had ever said that to Marty. Female, middle-aged, ever-so-slightly-frazzled politician – not a good look for a twelve-year-old boy. Emily was always saying she wanted to be Prime Minister too when she grew up, or PM as she insisted on calling it. He thought she probably would as well. She was definitely annoying enough.

On the TV a load of men and women in dreary, dark suits were sat in rows in the House of Commons, where Mum seemed to spend most of her time, listening to one bloke who was stood up, droning on about something or other. Mum was supposed to be there now, but she'd got delayed on the way back from a visit to some country or other, Marty couldn't even remember which one, so someone was standing in for her. From time to time the other MPs would either like what they heard or not like what they heard, and would do a weird kind of mumbly shout to either agree or disagree with him. It was mind-numbingly boring.

'Can't we turn over now?' Marty begged, before shovelling another forkful of rubbery, microwaved lasagne into his mouth.

'No,' snapped Emily. 'We need to watch this. The Chancellor is giving a very important speech.'

Marty had no idea who this Chancellor person was, or what he was on about, and he didn't want to either. He seemed to be banging on about some airport that he thought should be built, and if it wasn't built it would be very bad news, in his opinion. To be honest though, he sounded like the sort of person that if he told you you'd just won the lottery you'd end up thinking something terrible had happened, like a fat-berg had blocked up the sewers and your house had ended up six foot deep in raw sewage.

Marty didn't know who he was, but he had seen him around, arriving for meetings there at 10 Downing Street. The caption at the bottom of the screen said he was called Sir Jarvis Skelton, and he had a posh voice to match his posh name. He looked posh too, but there was something creepy about him as well.

'Which is exactly why I think we should turn over to something more interesting,' Marty argued. 'I think there's international paint drying on the other side, or maybe a repeat of a classic episode of celebrity grass growing.'

'Why don't you go and watch the paint in your bedroom if you're such a fan?' Emily told him.

'Why don't you go and…'

'That's enough you two,' interrupted Mum. 'Can't you both just get along for once? I do want to watch this. I should really have gone straight there from the airport. I'm sorry Marty, but once it's finished maybe we can see what else is on then.'

‘When this has finished you’ll be going back to work and Emily’s off to her meeting so I’ll be on my own again and I can watch whatever I want.’

‘Ooh, what will it be, Marty Farty, paint drying or grass growing?’ sneered Emily.

‘Oh shut up,’ he told her. ‘And don’t call me that.’

‘Both of you shut up!’ snapped Mum. ‘I can’t hear a word he’s saying now anyway. Why can’t you both just enjoy the nice meal and try to be civil to each other for five minutes. For goodness sake, it’s like being in a Cabinet meeting trying to keep control of you two.’

Marty and Emily both fell silent. He wondered if Mum was able to control her fellow MPs like that. He did wonder about pointing out that calling three microwaved lasagnes and a few bits of limp lettuce a ‘nice meal’ was pushing it a bit, but he didn’t think that would go down too well just then. Just like the lasagne wasn’t going down too well, as Mum had somehow managed to overcook it. She was definitely a better politician than she was a cook. It was pretty rare for the three of them to be eating tea together too, not that any of them were making the most of their quality family time.

If you were thinking for one moment that it sounded pretty cool, living in one of the most famous houses in the country, you'd be very wrong. It was dull. Dull, dull, dull. As dull as watching the Politics Channel 24/7 - unbelievably dull. The constant stream of boring, stuffy politicians and advisors who came to the house (which is the Prime Minister's office as well as her home) the endless security checks whenever anyone went in or out... it was all so tedious. If Marty wanted to just go to the shops, go for a burger or go out skateboarding, it all had to be planned in advance and cleared with security, and if he did go anywhere he had to have a security guard with him at all times. He kind of got why, but that didn't stop it being a right pain in the bum.

Not that Marty had any friends to go anywhere with anyway. He used to have some great mates back where they used to live, but he didn't like any of the other kids at the posh school he'd had to transfer to when they'd moved from their old home to London, and they didn't like him either. Put it this way, if your idea of fun was agonising over whether to go to Oxford like your mum or Cambridge like your dad, or boasting about how much your birthday party cost, or casually mentioning which celebrity happened to be on your family's yacht at the weekend, you'd probably have fitted in really well. It wasn't Marty's, so he didn't.

Emily seemed to like it at Number 10 though. She loved politics as much as Mum, and thought living in the heart of British government was great. She'd wanted to follow in Mum's footsteps for as long as Marty could remember, and living where she did, seeing and hearing what she did, was the best education she could possibly get, as she said *all* the time.

Marty sometimes wondered whether he should take more of an interest in what Mum was doing, like Emily did. She always knew exactly what was going on, what was at stake, but he just couldn't be bothered with it all.

On the TV someone seemed to be disagreeing with the Chancellor bloke now, talking about climate change, getting more mumbly shouts and causing other MPs to get up to demand their say.

'How do you think it's going to go Mum?' asked Emily.

'I really don't know,' Mum answered. 'Some MPs are convinced that the airport needs to be built and others are just as sure that it shouldn't because of climate change. What do you think?'

'I'm not sure either. I'm sure Parliament will make the right decision though.'

Marty pulled a face. What a creep. He didn't give his opinion, partly because he didn't have one and partly because no-one would care if he did. He was all for everyone doing everything they could to stop climate change of course, but he didn't really know anything about this airport, and he didn't want to either. He could have done without it being forced down his throat on the telly too, although, to be honest, it was a slight improvement on the lasagne.

The debate *finally* came to an end, and some woman with a microphone was now stood on the lawn outside the Houses of Parliament, explaining just how important it all was.

'Can we turn over now then?' Marty pleaded.

'We're still watching this,' answered Emily.

'But Mum said we could turn over when the speech finished.'

'Let's just see what the analysts have to say about it first, then we'll turn over.'

'Why would anyone care what anybody has to say about it?'

'Why would anyone care what *you* have to say about anything?'

He'd had enough. He grabbed the remote control off the table and pointed it at the TV, but before he could change the channel Emily snatched it off him.

'Give it back!' he yelled at her, trying to grab it back, but she held it out of his reach and laughed.

He grabbed her arm and her laugh turned into a screech.

'Marty! Get off her now!' shouted Mum, plucking the remote control away from both of them.

Now he'd definitely had enough.

'It's not fair!' he yelled. 'You always take *her* side. It's always about what you two want, never about what I want! You never listen to anything I say!'

'Marty…' started Mum, but he was already off and was running out of the room.

'I hate politics, I hate this house and I hate you two!'

'Marty!' she called after him, but he ignored her as he stomped back to his bedroom. He slammed the door behind him and hurled himself down onto his bed, fighting back tears of rage.

The gorilla-wrestler

Marty lay there, face down, for a few minutes. He half wondered if Mum would come after him, but he knew that she wouldn't. She was needed at some *hugely important* meeting back at the House of Commons after tea, and of course, she couldn't keep *them* waiting could she? Emily was going out to her Young Politicians meeting as well, so it was just him in the house this evening. Well, and the security staff.

Oh, and Larry the cat, who he hadn't noticed was sat on his windowsill, who'd probably been fast asleep until he'd made his dramatic entrance. Larry jumped down, then up onto the bed.

'It's alright for you,' Marty told him, tickling him between the ears. 'You get to come and go as you want. You even get the policemen outside the front door ringing the doorbell for you, don't you?'

He wasn't really their cat. He belonged to the house. Prime Ministers and their families came and went, but Larry stayed there. He even had an official title - Chief Mouser to the Cabinet Office. He seemed to know it was his house and everyone else was just a guest, although that's pretty much what all cats think about their houses.

Marty liked Larry, and he was glad Mum had insisted on living in Number 10 rather than Number 11, like most Prime Ministers with kids did. Next door had bigger bedrooms, but it didn't have Larry.

He turned over onto his back, turned his TV on and channel-hopped for a while. There was literally nothing on though. He thought about going on his phone or laptop, but he wasn't in the mood. He just needed something different to do.

He looked around his room for ideas. The one good thing about being the son of the Prime Minister was the gifts that you got from all sorts of world leaders and celebrities who visited Number 10. In the last year, since his mum became PM, he'd been given all sorts of things, from a space helmet by a Hollywood film director to a life-size inflatable crocodile (no, he had no idea either) by some aging rock-star he'd never heard of but who was apparently a big supporter of Mum's party.

He'd even been given a set of pens by the head of Britain's secret service, a nice old man who looked as unlike a spy as you could possibly imagine. Emily got one too and seemed delighted, but Marty hadn't been too impressed at first, until the man told him that one pen was a mega-powerful torch and the other was a state-of-the-art listening device. He suggested Marty could use them to 'have some fun with his friends'. Marty asked him if he could also have a sports car with a range of rocket-launchers, tyre-cutting blades and a smoke-screen device, but the man just chuckled and told him they were out of those.

The worst present he'd been given was a signed book about how great the US President was, written by the US President, given to him by the US President. Marty hadn't liked him much, and he certainly hadn't read his book.

He let out a giant sigh. Tomorrow was the first day of the summer holidays, which meant he had another six weeks of boredom to deal with. He used to love the summer holidays, before they moved there and he had to switch to his new school. Back when he used to have friends and was allowed out of the house to see them. He really missed them.

Marty was fed up of being in his room, and in the stupid house. It was all so unfair. He hadn't asked for his mum to get elected Prime Minister. He hadn't asked to move there and become a virtual prisoner. He felt like he just had to get out of there. He jumped up and stormed out of his room, down one floor to where all the meeting rooms were, and downstairs again. On the stairs there were photos and paintings of every British Prime Minister there'd ever been, like a kind of selfie-gallery, without the pouts or peace-signs of course.

'Boring old farts', Marty told them as he stomped past them, 'the lot of you.'

He was tempted to give them glasses and beards, fangs and sticky-out tongues, to make them a bit more interesting, but he didn't have a pen with him, and anyway, he didn't have time right then – he was leaving.

He ran over to the front door and tried to open it, but it was locked. He yanked at the door knob, and hammered on it with his fists as hard as he could.

'Let me out! Let me out!' he yelled furiously.

It didn't take long for someone to come and see what was going on. He heard the sound of footsteps thudding across the floor, and a shadow filled the hallway. The huge body of Leishman, Number 10's Head of Security, skidded to a halt next to him. The rumour was that he wrestled gorillas in his spare time, two at a time, although to be honest, why London Zoo would let him wrestle one, let alone two of their gorillas Marty wasn't sure. He looked like he could have though if they let him – he must have been nearly seven feet tall, and almost as wide, and no-one had any idea how his uniform didn't split under the strain of his gigantic muscles. He fixed Marty with the scowl that he permanently wore, his wild eyes boring into him, and a low growl emerged from deep within his fearsome, ginger beard.

More security guards arrived seconds later, not quite as big as Leishman, but all looking ready to tackle a major security alert. They looked a little disappointed to see that it was just the Prime Minister's slightly weedy (if he was honest) son. Marty wasn't in the mood to be intimidated by any of them though.

'Let-Me-Out-Now!' he demanded.

'I can't do that,' Leishman told him calmly, shaking his head. His voice had surprised Marty the first time he'd heard him speak. He sounded, well, normal. He'd expected him to have a giant voice to match his giant body, but he didn't.

'It's alright,' he told his colleagues. 'I've got this.'

They returned to wherever they'd been, and whatever they'd been doing, excitement over. He put his hand gently on Marty's arm to guide him away from the door, but Marty angrily shook it off.

'I'm going out,' he insisted.

'No can do. It's not been cleared with your mum.'

'You can't keep me locked up here.'

'It's for your own safety.'

'Yeah, right.'

'What do you think would happen if you stepped outside of that door anyway? You wouldn't be able to get past the security at the end of the street. And even if you did, we can't just let the son of the Prime Minister wander in and out as he pleases can we? You'd be hassled by the press and probably kidnapped by terrorists within seconds.'

'Really?'

'Definitely. Well, definitely the first bit, possibly the second bit. But it's not a risk we can take now, is it?'

Marty sighed. Leishman had a point, he supposed. It was still depressing being stuck in that prison though.

Leishman seemed to have had enough of talking in the hallway.

'Come on,' he said. 'Let's get you away from here.'

He put a hand firmly on Marty's back and ushered him towards the lift. Yes, they had a lift in their house. It was cool at first, but the novelty wore off pretty quickly. They stopped on the first floor, and Leishman led the way towards the Cabinet Office. It was the most important room in the building, where the Government had its meetings and basically ran the country.

It was also the most private. What was Leishman planning to do to him?

A way out?

Inside the Cabinet Office was quiet and calm. There was a portrait of someone important-looking above the fireplace and a huge, oval-shaped table in the middle of the room, already laid out for the next meeting with pads of paper, pens, glasses and big water jugs. You could feel the history and importance of the room. Everything looked old and important, from the chandelier hanging from the ceiling to the heavy curtains drawn across the huge windows at the back of the room, keeping the sun out and the room cool.

Leishman pulled a chair out from the table with a meaty hand and slowly lowered himself onto it. Despite being careful it still creaked under his bulk. Marty stayed where he was, wondering why they were in there. Did Leishman have some punishment in mind for him to make sure he didn't try to escape again? The security guard could tell Marty was nervous.

'Don't worry, I don't eat people,' he said. 'I might rip their arms off, or tie their legs together, or stick their feet in their ears. Never eat them though. Not any more anyway. Not since I became vegan.'

Marty thought he was probably joking, so managed a small, nervous laugh. He wasn't entirely sure though.

'It's Marty isn't it.'

It wasn't a question, but Marty nodded an answer anyway.

'Well Marty, how do you like living at Number 10?'

'Boring. Totally boring.'

'Yeah, I can see that this isn't the most exciting place for a twelve-year-old boy. You are twelve aren't you?'

'Yeah, it was my birthday last month.'

'Ah yes, I remember now. I had to keep an eye on your party. Your Mum invited all the kids of her fellow MPs around to the house, got a string quartet in to provide the music and the Downing Street chef prepared a selection of gourmet canapés.'

'Ugh, don't remind me', Marty grumbled. 'Worst birthday party ever.' They both shuddered together at the memory. Marty pulled out the chair next to Leishman and sat down.

'So, Marty,' said Leishman, trying to change the subject. 'Now you've had a look around the Cabinet Office, what do you think?'

'It's alright,' said Marty.

'Alright? Alright?! This is probably the most famous office in the country. One of the most important in the world. Just think of all the historic decisions that have been made by the country's greatest political minds over the years – Walpole, Pitt the Elder and Pitt the Younger, Disraeli, Gladstone, Lloyd-George…'

He noticed Marty's blank look.

'No? None of them?'

Marty shook his head.

'The Duke of Portland? The Earl of Shelburne? Don't tell me you've never heard of The Marquess of Rockingham?'

He kept on shaking his head.

'Jeez. What do they teach you in school these days?'

‘Are they the old farts on the stairs? They look totally boring.’

‘I guess you’ve got a point there. Politics is pretty boring if I’m honest.’

‘So is this house.’

‘Hm, I wouldn’t be so sure about that,’ Leishman said mysteriously. Marty waited for him to tell him more, but instead he said, ‘You know, it might be a bit boring in here too, but it is nice and quiet. If you ever want somewhere to do your homework, feel free. As long as there’s no-one else in here of course.’

‘Isn’t it usually locked?’ he asked.

‘Nope. No need. We check it first thing every morning but after that anyone can come and go as they please, once they’re inside Number 10 of course.’

‘Okay, well, I might do that. I have got some projects to do over the summer holidays. That’s about as much excitement as I’m going to get I suppose. As I’m not can’t even allowed to go outside.’

Leishman thought about this for a while, then leant in closer. He glanced around him before speaking.

‘You know,’ he said in a low voice, ‘I shouldn’t be telling you this, but, would a secret passage out of Number 10 be of interest to you at all?’

‘A secret passage?’ repeated Marty, matching his whisper, wondering again whether to believe him or not.

'A secret passage,' he repeated, waggling one eyebrow in a way that he probably thought was full of mystery. 'Of course, I couldn't possibly confirm or deny that it exists, but let's just say, if I was you, and I was going to look for it, I think there's a very strong possibility that I would find it, if you see what I mean.'

Marty nodded, even though he didn't.

'I think I might find myself looking for a hidden floor underneath the building, only accessible via the lift.'

'Via the lift?' Marty repeated again, louder than Leishman wanted, and the big man looked around anxiously again. Marty lowered his voice back down. 'Wait, what, there's a button in the lift marked "Hidden Floor" or "Secret Passage" or something is there?'

Leishman glanced round for a third time.

'No. Of course there's no button marked "Hidden Floor" or "Secret Passage". It would hardly be a secret then would it?' he tutted. 'No, you have to press *Number 10*. I mean, that's what I might try, if I was looking for it, you know.'

'Number 10? I don't remember there being a button with a 10 on it. And there aren't ten floors. Wouldn't people keep pressing it to see where it goes?'

Leishman just leant away and hauled himself to his feet. He gave Marty a theatrical wink, then strode towards the door.

'So, how are you supposed to press Number 10 if there isn't a Number 10 button?' Marty called after him.

Leishman paused at the door.

‘That’s something I’d have to work out isn’t it,’ he said, opening the door, ‘if I was looking for it. Which of course, I’m not. Because I haven’t actually confirmed that it exists. Have I?’

He frowned, as if he was trying to work out whether he had or not. Marty was glad it wasn’t just him who was confused.

‘Maybe it does, maybe it doesn’t. Then again,’ he added with another, even more theatrical wink, ‘maybe the world’s your *oyster*’. He left the room and closed the door behind him.

Marty stayed in his seat, thinking about what he’d just been told. Was Leishman joking about a secret passage? Surely he was. Marty thought he seemed the sort to enjoy a wind up. He’d probably keep a look out for him trying to work out how to make the lift go down to the secret floor, then come along and have a good laugh. Then again, he thought, he couldn’t see him as the sort to try to humiliate a twelve-year-old kid. Maybe he just thought it was a good story.

He’d had enough of the Cabinet Office for one day, so he said ‘see you later’ to the man in the portrait above the fireplace, opened the door and headed back to his room.

He couldn’t help wondering though, was there really a secret passage?

The secret passage

The next morning it was sunny but a bit chilly. Marty got up late, got himself some Coco-Pops, left the kitchen quickly when his sister arrived, showered, got dressed, then remembered that he had absolutely nothing else planned for the rest of the day. Mum had gone off to work long before he'd got up, and Emily was now nowhere to be seen. The rest of the house was still busy as people raced around, looking ever so important and stressed, on their way to meetings and whatever else they did. He wasted some time on his laptop, but he was soon desperate again for something more interesting to do.

It looked really nice outside. He just wanted to go out to do something, anything to get out of the stuffy old house. There was a garden at the back of the house, but there was nothing in it really, so he didn't really fancy that. He found himself wondering about the secret passage that Leishman had told him about the night before. Had he just been winding him up, or did it really exist? He was sure it didn't, but he didn't have anything better to do. It wouldn't hurt to check it out at least, would it?

He grabbed his wallet, a cap and sunglasses, just in case he did end up in the sunshine outside, and his secret service pen that was really a torch, which he thought might come in handy in a secret passage. He made his way downstairs to the lift, which only went up to the first floor, not the second floor where they lived. There was someone there waiting for it though, holding a huge stack of folders, so he just walked on past. He waited for a minute around the corner, then looked back. She'd gone, and he went back and pressed the button to call the lift. After a few seconds it arrived. The door opened, and there was no-one inside, so he stepped in and the door rattled shut behind him.

He looked at the panel of buttons and tried to remember what Leishman had told him. 'Press number 10' he had said, but, just as Marty had pointed out, there was no number 10 button, just numbers 0 and 1, plus buttons to open and close the door and an emergency button. He must have been making it up. Marty was about to press the button to open the door and leave when he had a thought. There wasn't a number 10, but there was a 1 and a 0. You could put them together to look like ten. He tried pressing the 1, then the 0. The lift started moving downwards, and he got a bit excited, but that didn't last long as the lift doors opened onto the ground floor. Then he tried pressing the 1 and the 0 together. The doors closed and the lift started moving down again, and this time it kept going down.

Eventually the doors opened again, onto a room he'd never seen before. It was a small, concrete space, about twice the size of the lift, completely empty apart from a single light-bulb hanging from the ceiling. Opposite the lift door was another, solid-looking door. Marty walked over to it and took a closer look. Surely this wasn't actually it? He pulled at it and the door smoothly swung open.

He couldn't believe it. Leishman had been telling the truth. The light from behind him lit up the first few metres, but after that it was pitch black. He dug out his pen/torch and switched it on.

He was hoping to be greeted by the kind of secret passage you'd read about in an adventure story – dark and creepy and spooky. He should have realised that one built by government types would be nothing like that though. There were no scuttling rats, no echoes of water dripping into inky-black puddles, no cobwebs to startle you as they tickled your face, and no whistling winds sounding eerily like somebody moaning and groaning. It was dark, but other than that it was just a bland, grey, concrete corridor, silent apart from the echo of Marty shouting "hello!", to see if there was an echo. No imagination, politicians. Still, he was too excited about sneaking out to let it bother him.

He took a step forward, then stopped. He could get into serious trouble for this, couldn't he? What if Mum found out he'd sneaked out? He was only going for a quick look though, just to see where it went. He'd be back before she had any idea he'd been out. He took another step forward, and let the door close behind him with a loud clunk that echoed along the passage. He hoped he hadn't just locked himself in. He took a deep breath and started walking.

After about a hundred metres he came to a bend in the passage. He peered around, to check that the spooky stuff wasn't lying in wait for him there, but it was just more of the same. There were another couple of hundred metres still to go before what looked like another door at the end, which got bigger and bigger as he got closer to it (as things in the distance tend to do when you walk towards them).

After a couple of minutes he came to a door, which looked exactly like the one he'd just come through. He turned the handle and gave it one a push, and again, it swung smoothly open. There was another, small concrete room, identical to the one he'd just left, with a lift door and a call button. He turned his torch off and pressed the button. Nothing happened. He pressed it again. Still nothing happened. Surely he wasn't going to get stuck now. Finally, after another couple of presses, he thought he could hear something. After a few seconds there was a click, and the doors slid open. He stepped into the lift and looked at the control panel. This one had slightly different options, 0 and -1. He tried 0. The door closed and the lift started upwards. He wondered where it would arrive.

A few seconds later he found out. The doors opened, and he got out as a crowd of people pushed their way in. It didn't take him long to realise he was in a station. A busy station, with lots of business people hurrying around with briefcases and laptop bags. It seemed really noisy after the quiet of the secret passage. He knew he should really have turned around and gone back home, but it seemed a shame not to at least have a quick look outside. He looked for the exit, and saw that he couldn't get to it without going through the ticket barrier.

One problem though - he didn't have a ticket. He rummaged around in his wallet, hoping that his old Oyster card was there, and was relieved to find it, hiding behind some old receipts and a chewing gum wrapper. He hadn't used it since Mum became Prime Minister (the Oyster card, not the chewing gum wrapper), when they used to visit London rather than living there, but he was sure there was still some credit on it. So that was what Leishman meant when he said the world was his oyster. Could he not have just said 'Make sure you take your Oyster card'?

He approached the barrier, scanned his card, and breathed a sigh of relief when it opened. He headed outside, blinking in the bright sunlight.

Marty started walking away, then sensibly remembered to check to see what station it was so he could find his way back. The sign above the doorway said 'Westminster Underground Station'. That made sense. It was the closest one to Downing Street. He wondered how many thousands of people used it every day, with no idea that it housed a secret tunnel into the most closely guarded house in the country.

He realised that he had no idea where he was going, or what he was going to do. He put his sunglasses on and headed away from Big Ben and the Houses of Parliament, which were at the back of the station, keeping his head down just in case Mum happened to be looking out of one of the windows, even though he knew it was highly unlikely, and walked alongside the Thames for a while. He watched the tourist boats going up and down the river, and was happy to not just be stuck indoors. When he got to the next bridge he could hear noises to his left, so he decided to see what was going on, forgetting that he was only supposed to be having a quick look around.

As he walked towards it they started to get louder and louder, and he could make out drums and whistles, and people shouting. He reached the end of the road. It was getting really loud now, and rammed with people.

It was when he turned the corner though that the noise really hit him. He realised that he was at Trafalgar Square, but he'd never seen it looking like it did then.

Jumi

Trafalgar Square was packed full of thousands of people of all ages and backgrounds – old, young, men, women, every skin colour you can think of. Men with beards, men without beards, women without beards, even a woman with a beard (actually a man wearing a dress Marty realised after a second glance). There was long hair, short hair, braided hair, brightly coloured hair, shaved heads, bald heads, heads covered with hats, caps, bandannas and head scarves. Painted faces, smiling faces, determined faces, hopeful faces. There were people with flags, and people holding banners, people playing guitars, people wheeling bikes and people wheeling their wheelchairs. People were cheering, chanting, blowing whistles and banging drums. There was a makeshift stage with a microphone, and a man was speaking to the crowd through giant speakers powered by solar panels. Quite a few people had brought their dogs with them, someone had brought a pig on a lead, and there was even a woman in the corner playing a piano that she'd got from somewhere. All around them were policemen and women, many of them smiling and laughing with the crowd, and loads of people taking photos. He'd never seen anything like it.

He picked his way through the crowd, amazed by the people, the colour and the noise. He was glad he had his cap and shades on, just to be sure that no-one recognised him. Something told him that anyone related to a leading politician probably wouldn't be exactly popular with protesters, whatever they were protesting about. He noticed that the banners all had 'Eco Now' or 'EN' printed on them, but he had no idea what that was.

'This is great isn't it?' said a voice beside him. He turned to see whose voice it was, and saw a girl, about his age, with a mass of frizzy hair, a purple t-shirt with that EN logo on it, cut-off denim shorts and red canvas trainers.

'Um, yeah. Really great,' he agreed.

'Haven't seen you before,' she carried on. 'Is this your first one?'

'Um, yeah,' he agreed again.

'Do you answer every question 'um, yeah'?'

'Um, yeah,' he answered again, adding a smile to show that he'd got the joke. She smiled too.

'I'm Jumi,' she told him.

'Marty,' he said, and kicked himself for not thinking to give her a fake name so she didn't work out who he was. It didn't seem to cross her mind though that he might be someone vaguely well-known. Maybe he was being a bit big-headed thinking that anyone would have any idea who he was, even if he didn't have his cunning disguise.

'So, your first Eco Now protest. I'm not sure I can even remember my first one,' said Jumi, as they started walking slowly through the crowd.

'Have you been to lots then?' he asked her.

'Oh yeah, loads. Me and my Dad. He's over there,' she said, pointing towards a group of people listening to the man speaking on the stage. 'Who are you here with?'

'Oh, I came on my own. My Mum's, er, busy today, and it's really not my sister's thing.'

'Don't they care about what's happening to our planet?'

'Um, well, no, I'm not sure they do really.'

‘That’s terrible. So many people just don’t care. They just want to make money, drive their massive cars and fly around the world on stupid, great polluting planes all the time. That’s what today’s about.’

‘What?’

‘Planes. Well, airports. They’re trying to build a new airport in the countryside, just outside London. Haven’t you heard about it? Winston Churchill Airport they want to call it.’

‘Winston Churchill Airport? World War 2 Prime Minister Winston Churchill?’ That was one of the few things Marty could remember from history lessons, and Churchill was the only person he’d recognised from the old farts on the stairs yesterday as well. He thought he’d better not mention that though.

‘Why are they going to call it that?’

‘Dad says it's so that they can call anyone who's against it unpatriotic. He’s probably right.’

Marty wondered whether anyone would ever want to name an airport after Mum. That would be weird – “Ladies and gentlemen we will shortly be beginning our approach to Charlotte Marsh airport, please return to your seats and fasten your seatbelts”. Really weird.

‘If they build it it’ll destroy Chumley Woods,’ she added. ‘A whole load of ancient woodland will be gone forever, not to mention all the extra CO2 from the planes. That’s why Eco Now are trying to get it stopped.’

Marty suddenly realised that this must have been what they'd been talking about on the Politics Channel. He wished he'd paid more attention so he could say something intelligent and meaningful about it.

'Wow,' he said instead. 'That sounds terrible.'

'It is.'

'So, how will you stop it?'

'Well, we need to make the politicians wake up and realise what's going on.'

'Politicians?'

'Yeah. They're the ones who are going to be making the decision, so they're the ones who have to understand all the damage the airport will do if it gets built.'

'Won't they just try to build it somewhere else though?'

'Maybe, but if they do we'll just have to start again. We *have* to start putting the planet first.'

'Yeah, I suppose so. But do you think they'll listen?'

'They've got to. We have to make them.'

'Um, which politicians, in particular, are going to decide about the airport?' he asked.

'All MPs I think, but it kind of depends of what the Prime Minister tells them,' said Jumi, telling him exactly what he'd suspected.

'Oh, right,' Marty said, grimacing.

'What?' Jumi glared at him. 'Don't you think we can make them listen?'

'No, it's not that, it's just. Well. Actually, they do tend to ignore what people want don't they, MPs?'

'But Marty, look at all the people here today. This is happening all over the country right now. And it's going to keep on happening. They can't ignore us forever.'

'I hope you're right,' he told her.

'Have you got any better ideas?' she asked him.

He thought about that before answering. Was there anything *he* could do? In theory he had direct access to the main decision-maker, his mum, but in reality, she never listened to him when he was telling her what he'd done at school, so she wasn't going to listen to him about this. And anyway, did he really want to get involved?

'Not at the moment,' he told her. 'I'll give it some thought. I would like to come to your next rally though, if you've got another one planned.' It would give him something to do at least, and he liked the idea of seeing Jumi again.

'Cool. That's a start anyway,' she said with a smile. 'Give me your number and I'll message you.' He gave her his number, and she gave him hers.

Together they wandered over towards the stage and listened for a bit. A serious-looking, middle-aged man with trendy glasses and a shaved head was passionately telling the crowd how much damage to the planet cutting down the woods to build an airport would do, pretty much as Jumi just had. He was getting a lot of cheers.

'They call him the Newt,' Jumi told him. 'He's one of the organisers.'

'The Newt? Why the Newt?'

'Apparently there's this type of rare newt that if they find it anywhere no-one can build there until they can find a new home for the newts. They reckon he's stopped as many developments as the real newts have. You know what newts are, right?'

'Like frogs, but longer.'

'Basically.'

'OK. There aren't any…'

'Newts at Chumley Woods? No, unfortunately not. We've checked.'

'That's a shame,' said Marty weakly.

'You might have seen his YouTube channel? It's worth a look. He knows everything about conservation, climate change, government corruption, that kind of thing. He posted one the other day all about how the Prime Minister isn't taking climate change seriously and seems happy to let the planet die around us.'

'Right, OK. Maybe I'll take a look.' Awkward.

On the stage the Newt was still getting big cheers. He was a passionate speaker and seemed to be very popular with the other protesters, who he was urging not to give up and telling them that the future of the planet was in their hands. He was also very critical of politicians for failing to do anything to help and said there was too much corruption getting in the way of change. They listened as he talked about "the point of no return" and how that meant everyone really, *really* had to act now. It was pretty inspirational stuff, if you were into that sort of thing.

'I'm hungry. Are you hungry?' Jumi suddenly asked him. She'd probably heard it before if she was a regular at these rallies.

'Yeah, a bit.'

'Let's get something to eat then,' she said, heading towards a man cooking food on a portable barbeque. He looked like he was about a hundred, and Marty wondered if he'd been around when the ancient woodland was planted, but he was dancing around to the music as he grilled the burgers and split pitta breads. Jumi seemed to know him.

'Hi Art,' she greeted him.

'Oh, hi Jumi,' he grinned back. 'Who's your friend?'

'This is Marty.'

'Wotcha Marty. Can I do you a plant-based burger?'

Marty wasn't sure exactly what that was, but it sounded better than overcooked frozen lasagne, so he said yes please. Art flipped a burger off the grill into a pitta bread, threw in some salad and sauce and proudly handed it to him. Art and Jumi watched him expectantly. It was actually delicious.

'Mmm,' he mumbled, trying to stop the sauce from running down his chin. He swallowed, realising that he actually was quite hungry. 'That's the nicest thing I've eaten in ages.'

They both looked suitably pleased, and Art started making another for Jumi.

'Even vegans can eat these you know,' Jumi told him.

'Are you vegan then?' he asked her.

'No. Veggie, but not vegan. I'm not quite ready to give up ice-cream yet.'

Art finished Jumi's burger and passed it to her, just as proudly as Marty's.

'Thanks Art,' said Jumi, as they headed back into the crowd.

'Yeah, thanks Art,' Marty shouted back in between mouthfuls.

The crowd was starting to thin out now, and it was getting less noisy.

'That's pretty much it for today,' said Jumi. 'Everyone will be heading off soon.'

He popped the last of his burger into his mouth.

'Oh, OK. I'd probably better be going soon anyway.'

'Where do you live?' she asked him. That wasn't as easy to answer as it should have been.

'Not far,' he told her. 'I need to get back to Westminster station, then it's about ten minutes from there,' which was true. He just wouldn't be getting home from there in the way she would assume.

She accepted that without asking him to be any more specific, which was a relief as he didn't want to have to lie to her.

'OK. Well, I'll go and find my Dad then. I'll let you know when the next rally is.'

'Great,' said Marty. 'Right, I'd better go then. Nice to meet you Jumi.'

'You too,' she said.

He turned away and starting walking back to the station, thinking that the summer holidays might not be too bad after all. He thought a few of those protesters seemed a bit weird, but Jumi was cool. If it meant he could hang out with her, he was happy to pretend to be an eco warrior.

Coco-Pops and ketchup

When Marty got back to the station he used his Oyster card to go straight back through the ticket barrier, then looked for the lift. There were some tourists waiting for it, so he hung back and waited for them to go. When the lift returned he stepped forward and got in, but a family jumped in behind him before the door closed. Obviously he couldn't go to the secret floor with them there, so he just pressed -1 and pretended to get out after them onto the platform. Once they'd gone he got straight back in, and the door closed with him now the only person in the lift.

He pressed -1 and 0, hoping that the minus didn't make any difference, and waited, but nothing happened. He tried again, but still nothing happened. This wasn't good. Why wasn't it working? He tried not to panic, and tried -1 and 0 again. Still the lift refused to budge. Maybe it wasn't -1 and 0 that made it work, but there weren't any other buttons to try. Then the doors opened and he saw a man with a pushchair waiting to get in, so he got out to think about what to do next.

He couldn't be stuck there, could he? He could always walk back to Downing Street, he was sure he could find the way, but there was no way security would let him through the huge gates at the end of the street. He could imagine them, checking with their colleagues to see if he'd been let out, and of course they'd say he hadn't, and they wouldn't believe he was who he said he was, even if he took his cunning disguise off. Also, if he did finally manage to get in, Mum was bound to find out what he'd done and he'd be grounded forever.

He watched all the people on the platform, waiting for the next train, and tried to keep calm. What could he do? Leishman would let him in, but he didn't work on the gates and Marty had no way of getting in touch with him. Just as he was about to panic he spotted another lift a bit further along. That got his hopes up again. Maybe that was the one to the secret floor and he'd been trying the wrong one. He ran over to it and pressed the button. The doors opened immediately, and he got in. The second the doors closed he tried pressing -1 and 0, and breathed a huge sigh of relief as he felt the lift start to move downwards.

He got out when it stopped, and was back in the small, concrete room. He wasn't home and dry yet though, as the door to the passage was protected by a key pad, with letters from A to Z. Couldn't Leishman have given him a bit more detail about this? What would the combination be? He assumed it would be a word rather than random letters, although he had no way of knowing if that was right. If it was just random he had no chance of guessing it, but if it was a word, maybe he could.

First he tried T-E-N, then when that didn't work he tried N-U-M-B-E-R-T-E-N, but that didn't work either. What else could it be? He tried P-M, then P-R-I-M-E-M-I-N-I-S-T-E-R, but they also did nothing. How about their surname – M-A-R-S-H? No. Surely it wasn't something ridiculously easy, like A-B-C, or X-Y-Z? Nope. He remembered something he'd read about people using their kids' names as passwords, so he tried M-A-R-T-Y, then E-M-I-L-Y, but they didn't work either, and neither did Mum's name C-H-A-R-L-O-T-T-E.

It looked like he was stuck. He gave the door a kick, which hurt his foot and was totally pointless. He remembered from coming through it on the way here, it was thick and solid, as you'd expect when you remembered where it led to. It had probably been built to withstand sledgehammers and explosives, so a 12-year-old boy wasn't about to kick his way through it.

Marty sat down on the ground with his back against the door. What was he going to do now? He felt like Larry, sat outside the front door to Number 10, waiting for a policeman to let him in, although he wasn't about to be let in by a kind constable. That's when it hit him. Larry! He jumped up and quickly typed in L-A-R-R-Y. That didn't work though. Maybe he was wrong. Or maybe it was Larry's official title rather than his name. He tried again – M-O-U-S-E-R. There was a click, and a clunk, and the door edged open. Marty pulled it fully open and was unbelievably relieved to enter the passageway.

The door swung shut behind him, and he was in pitch blackness, but he found his torch-pen in his pocket and switched it on. He hurried onwards, and in a few minutes he was back in the little room at the other end, calling the lift. It quickly arrived, and he pressed 1 to get back to floor below theirs. Soon he was back on the landing outside his room, amazed that he could be so pleased to be back inside Number 10. His relief was short-lived though, as he saw Emily come out of her room.

'Where have you been?' she demanded.

'Nowhere,' he told her.

'Yes you have. You haven't been in your room or anywhere else in the building. And why have you got your cap and sunglasses on?'

He'd forgotten to take them off in his anxiety to get back in.

'Oh, I've been in the garden,' he lied, hoping she hadn't checked there.

'In the garden?'

'Yeah.'

Emily looked like she was trying to decide whether to believe him or not. Then she peered at her brother closely.

'What's that on your chin?'

Marty remembered the burger sauce that he'd dribbled at the rally. He must have missed a bit. It seemed barely real that he'd even been there now.

'Oh that. That must be some ketchup from breakfast.'

'I thought you had Coco-Pops for breakfast this morning.'

'Um, yeah. Coco-Pops with ketchup.'

'Ugh. You're disgusting,' she told him, and marched back to her room.

There were some advantages to your sister thinking you're weird, he decided. His secret was safe, for now at least. He wondered what Emily would say if she found out he was now pretending to be an eco warrior. Actually, he knew exactly what she'd say, and it wouldn't be nice. He'd just have to make sure she didn't find out.

The vampire MP

Marty struggled to get to sleep that night. Maybe he was still excited from his mini-adventure, or maybe it was because he'd been trying, unsuccessfully, to think of something he could do to help the Eco Now cause and impress Jumi.

He had eventually got to sleep, and when he woke up the next day the weather had changed completely. The bright sun had been replaced by pouring rain, and it was chilly, dark and pretty miserable for a so-called summer's day. According to his phone there was a thunderstorm on the way too. It was all pretty depressing, and he was as fed-up again now as he had been before he'd got out and met Jumi.

With nothing to do again he thought about making use of the secret passage, now that he knew how to get in and out of it, but he couldn't think of anywhere indoors in London that he wanted to go, and anyway, he'd have got soaked as soon as he left the station, which he couldn't be bothered with. Instead, he just hung about in his bedroom for a bit, playing on his computer, until he was bored of that too.

It really was the worst summer holidays ever. He sighed. He was so bored he thought he might as well get some of his summer homework done. That's how bored he was. He was just getting it out when there was a knock on his door.

'Hello?' he answered.

'I need to clean your room now please,' called a voice through the door.

'It's fine, it doesn't need doing,' Marty told them.

'I'm sorry, I have to do it,' the voice insisted. Marty was a bit annoyed, but he knew the cleaner had been told to clean it every week. It was as if someone thought twelve-year-old boys couldn't keep their bedrooms clean and tidy (as if). Anyway, he thought, if they didn't do it now they'd just keep bugging him until they had.

'OK, just a minute,' he shouted back, grabbing his folder and pencil case in a strop, and he opened the door to let the cleaner in as he went out. It wasn't like there weren't any other rooms in the house he could work in. He went downstairs to find one, but all the doors were closed, and when he put his ear to them they all sounded like they had meetings going on in them. Apart from the Cabinet Office – he couldn't hear anyone in there.

He wondered whether it was really OK if he worked in there. Leishman had told him it was, but was he telling the truth? He'd been right about the secret passage though hadn't he?

Marty opened the door a crack and looked in. It was empty, like he thought. He went in and chose a seat. There were plenty to choose from, and he sat down at the one closest to the window, furthest from the door. He opened his folder and put his pencil case on the table next to it. It was, to be fair, a pretty impressive place to do your homework, if you had to do homework anywhere.

He looked through his folder. He had some history, geography, science and English to do. He was supposed to do some research and a couple of essays before he went back to school in September. That was ages away though. He didn't need to start it just yet. Maybe he'd leave it for a while. It did feel though like the bloke in the portrait above the fire was watching him though, looking down disapprovingly at his lack of progress.

'Yeah? What?' Marty asked him. The man in the portrait didn't answer, unsurprisingly.

Marty put his folder down and gazed out of the window for a while. It was still chucking it down, but the thunderstorm hadn't started yet.

He was interrupted by the sound of the door opening behind him. A man he recognised entered the room. It was the man who was giving the tedious speech on the TV, the Chancellor, Marty thought they called him. Sir somebody-or-other Skelton? As the man stared at Marty, looking surprised that he was there, Larry started to stalk in past him into the room, but Skelton aimed a kick at him. Fortunately Larry was way too quick for him though and he ran back out with an angry yowl.

The man was tall and overly thin and wore a dark blue, old-fashioned-looking suit and a dark black tie. He looked like he probably disliked garlic and sunlight *a lot*, and his idea of a tasty snack was something he sucked out of someone's neck in the middle of the night. Were the un-dead allowed to serve as Members of Parliament? Marty suddenly wished very much that he was somewhere else. Anywhere else.

The Chancellor peered at Marty over the top of his round glasses like he was something smelly that a dog had just deposited on the carpet.

'Oh, a *child,*' he sneered. 'One would have thought one would be free from snivelling, screeching, snotty nosed brats in here, but one would obviously be sadly mistaken. You belong to the PM don't you? You really shouldn't be in here you know.' It wasn't a question, but he stared at Marty as if he was expecting an answer.

'Ah, um, no, I was just...' Marty started, struggling to speak and feeling very hot under the collar.

'Yes?' prompted Skelton.

'I was just... um, doing some homework.'

'Homework eh?' said Skelton. 'Don't you have a little room of your own where you could do whatever it is you need to do without disturbing the important business of Her Majesty's Government, hm?'

'Um, yes. I guess I do,' Marty stammered.

'You guess? You guess you do? Don't you know? Why do you need to guess? Let's be a little more decisive shall we?'

'Oh, well, yes, I have, I do. I just...'

'Yes?'

'I just... I'm just going to... go.' Marty legged it past him, out of the Cabinet Office, just as his mum and some other MPs were going in.

'Marty?' she called after him. 'Are you OK?'

'Fine!' he shouted, without looking back, and he raced into his room and slammed the door behind him, just as the thunder and lightning started. Fortunately, the cleaner had finished.

Marty breathed a sigh of relief. He don't know what it was about him, but that man made his skin crawl. He decided he'd do his best not to run into him anywhere in the house again.

It was only then that he realised that in his rush to leave the Cabinet Office he'd left his folder and pencil case in there. He wondered how long their meeting was going to last. He needed them if he was going to get any homework done, but he really didn't want to risk bumping into Skelton again.

Then he had a brainwave. One of the pens in his pencil case was the listening bug he'd been given by the secret service guy. He could activate it via his laptop and listen in to hear when they finished, then go and get his stuff. He turned on his laptop and started up the app that went with the bug. It took a couple of minutes, but it worked. He could hear everything they were saying.

The airport plan

Not that it was the slightest bit interesting.

Marty half listened as the meeting rambled on. They were talking about something involving the EU, the USA and China, but he couldn't understand much of what they were saying. Emily would have done. Marty knew she'd have loved listening in on it, although she'd probably also freak out if she knew what he was doing.

The meeting went on and on, just like the speech on the TV had, going from one boring topic to the next.

'Next on the agenda,' Marty heard his mum say, 'is a new initiative from a charity called Healthy Body Healthy Mind that's looking for Government support. It looks very worthwhile from what I've seen so far. I'm looking for someone to get involved with them, give them support and assistance where we can. Is anyone interested?'

There was complete silence. Mum waited until it was clear no-one was going to volunteer.

'Well, that's a shame. I'll just have to tell all of the stars from the worlds of film, TV, music and sport who have already signed up to be ambassadors for the programme that we're not interested.'

'Ah, now, hold on a minute Prime Minister,' said a lady who sounded like she either had a heavy cold or very bad hay-fever. 'If it's got the word "healthy" in the title it's got to be something I as Health Secretary should be in charge of.'

'Oh no you don't Henrietta,' chipped in another lady. 'This is clearly something that my Department for Culture and Sport should be looking at.'

'No way, Gurinda, you're not taking this one,' said the first lady, who Marty decided to call Hayfever Henrietta. 'You get to hang out with plenty of celebrities in your role as it is. Give someone else a chance.'

Marty realised then why they were all suddenly so keen to get involved. A chance to mix with actors, singers and sportspeople, and presumably get the public to see them rubbing shoulders with the stars. Politicians loved that sort of thing, didn't they? Even he knew that.

'I think I should be involved as well, Prime Minister,' said a man firmly.

'What on earth has this got to do with the Department for Environment, Food and Rural Affairs Clive?'

'Food, Gurinda, food! You've got to have healthy food if you want to be healthy. This is a job for Clivey B, the C Dog, C Diddy. You know what I mean?'

'No!' snapped another man angrily. 'None of us has any idea what you mean, as usual, Clive. And anyway, this has clearly got the Home Office written all over it.'

'That's ridiculous Alan,' a third man told him. 'You're talking rubbish. You're all talking rubbish. This is clearly something that I should be in charge of.'

'The Foreign Secretary?!' Alan spluttered. Alan seemed to be very angry.

'This is clearly a very high profile matter that needs to be handled by someone who knows what he's doing and isn't going to make a complete mess of it,' the man who was obviously the Foreign Secretary insisted.

'Yeah right,' scoffed the man they'd called Clive. 'And that's you is it Barry, the man who almost lost his seat in the last election after he called a voter "the stupidest man in Britain" when he thought his microphone was off?'

'Well I was clearly wrong anyway wasn't I? No-one else is going to win the title "the stupidest man in Britain" with *you* around are they?'

'OK, OK, that's enough everyone,' Mum told them, trying to get the conversation back on track. Clive wasn't finished with Barry yet though.

'Well if you were in charge you probably wouldn't even turn up, like when you missed that debate last month because it clashed with the final of Celebrity Paradise Island.'

'I'll have you know I have never missed a debate because of Celebrity Paradise Island.'

'Ah, not denying you watch it though are you I notice.'

'I may have seen it, once or twice, but only as research you understand.'

'Quiet!' Marty heard his mum shout.

That shut them up. For a bit anyway. Were these really the people running the country? It was very hard to believe.

'That's quite enough of that thank you very much,' Mum continued. He could see now what she meant about him and Emily being like a Cabinet meeting when they argued. 'I'll decide later who I think should get involved with the initiative. Let's move on now. Alan, could you present your report on the latest hospital spending review please.'

Alan started to give his report, sounding more monotonous than angry now, and Marty soon started to doze off.

* * *

He woke up with a start when he heard raised voices again. Was the meeting still going? It sounded like they were squabbling again.

'Hallelujah, I think she's finally seen the light,' Barry was saying.

'I've been seeing the light for the last hour and a half thank you very much, reflecting off your bald bonce Barry. Could somebody close the curtains please?' sneered Gurinda.

'If you were able to see anything out of those jam-jar glasses of yours you'd realise that the curtains were already closed, speccy.'

How old were these people, wondered Marty? Six? Mind you, he was going to call them Bald Barry and Glasses Gurinda from now on.

‘Guys, guys. Just chill,’ said Clive.

‘Guys? Chill? Will you please stop trying to be “down wiv the kidz” all the bloomin’ time Clive?’

It was a fair point actually. Clive did seem desperate to be the cool one. Cool Clive, thought Marty.

‘Oh, forget it,’ snapped Mum. ‘I’ll do it myself. Right, what’s next on the agenda? The long term potential impact of artificial intelligence on the UK employment market... I think we might skip that one for now. OK then, Winston Churchill Airport.’

Marty had been about to turn it off as he really didn’t think he could take any more, but that got his attention. That was the airport Jumi and Eco Now had been protesting about.

‘I saw on the news there were more protests about that all over the country yesterday,’ said Angry Alan.

‘Idiots,’ muttered a voice that sent a shiver down Marty’s spine. It was Skelton, who’d been suspiciously quiet up until then. He hadn’t been desperate for the chance to meet some celebrities, and no-one had thrown any childish insults his way, Marty noticed. They were probably scared he’d try to bite their necks if they did. ‘All this fuss about climate change. It’s all a con you realise. None of it’s been proved.’

‘You can’t possibly say that,’ complained Cool Clive. ‘There’s a shed-load of a lot of evidence to support it out there.’

'Balderdash! Fake news,' declared Skelton.

'We do need to consider the potential impact of increasing flight numbers on carbon emissions,' Marty was pleased to hear his mum say.

'Not to mention bulldozing a huge area of natural habitat.'

'And all those car journeys for people getting to the airport.'

'So you'd be happy to see job losses would you?' Skelton came back with. 'Thousands of jobs could be lost if we fall behind the rest of the world. Other countries are building new airports and new runways. They're encouraging business. What sort of message does it send out if we're not? Businesses will choose to go elsewhere and jobs will be lost. I'm certainly not going to be the one to tell the public they've lost their jobs because we wanted to save a poxy little forest and a few mangy squirrels.'

'It will cost us votes,' Hayfever Henrietta agreed with him.

'It's grossly unfair that air travel gets the blame for this so-called climate emergency anyway,' continued Skelton. 'The airline industry has been doing sterling work in reducing carbon emissions, and in the future we're going to have electric planes.'

'"In the future? In the future?" When exactly will that be Sir Jarvis? It'll be too late by then.'

'People need connectivity Clive. Building the airport is just common sense. Hard-working families are fed up with the political elite telling them they can't go on holiday.'

'Nobody's telling them they can't go on holiday.'

'Holidays. That's a point,' snuffled Henrietta. 'I've got to travel right the way from one side of London to the other when I go on holiday to Bali in a few weeks. It would be far easier for me if Winston Churchill Airport was built.'

'In a few weeks! How long do you think it takes to build an airport?'

'I wasn't thinking of *this* holiday, you prize numpty. I was thinking of *future* holidays.'

'Don't you call me a numpty.'

'I didn't. I called you a *prize* numpty.'

Marty shook his head in disbelief. Were these idiots really going to make such a huge decision just because it would make their own holiday plans easier?

'Right!' shouted Mum. 'I think we've heard enough. Can we just see – who would be for and against the airport if the vote was today? Barry?'

'For.'

'Henrietta?'

'For.'

'Alan?'

'Against.'

'Sir Jarvis?'

'For, of course.'

'Gurinda?'

'Against.'

'Clive?'

‘Against.’

‘Oh, this is ridiculous,’ complained Skelton.

‘Three for, three against at the moment then,’ said Mum. ‘I’m yet to make up my mind.’

‘Are you people all imbeciles?’ Skelton was clearly not happy.

‘Thank you, Sir Jarvis,’ she told him sharply. Marty could sense him silently fuming. ‘Alright, let’s move on for now. We’ll discuss this again at our next meeting no doubt.’

Marty was sure he heard his mum sigh. Who could blame her? He couldn’t take any more either, so he turned his laptop off.

Had he just overheard something important though? Was it something Eco Now could use to stop the airport being built?

The point of no return

Marty waited about an hour, then turned his laptop back on to see if they were still going. It was all quiet in there. He sneaked back down and into the Cabinet Office to get his stuff back, desperately hoping he wouldn't bump into Skelton in the corridor. Thankfully he didn't. His pencil case and folder were exactly where he had left them, and it looked like no-one had touched them.

As he picked them up he wondered what he should do about what he'd just heard. Should he tell Jumi that most of the Government seemed to be supporting the airport, if only to make it easier for them to go on holiday? At least three of them were against it, and his mum might decide to be too, unless somebody or something convinced her it was a good idea. Would that be enough though?

And he could get into big trouble if he told anyone, couldn't he? He was sure there were laws against giving away the Government's secrets. He might even be arrested for spying, and there was no way Mum could carry on being Prime Minister if her son was a spy. He wasn't sure knowing what he knew would actually help them much anyway. Maybe it was better if he said nothing and hoped for the best.

He returned to his room, and checked his phone. There was a message from Jumi waiting for him. She'd sent him links to some videos about Eco Now and what they were protesting about. He made himself comfy and started to watch them.

Marty was soon watching in horror as the rainforests were burned, and as the seas and oceans filled with plastic waste. He cried as an orang-utan tried desperately to stop a bulldozer destroying her home, as turtles got caught up nets and drowned, as starving polar bears searched in vain for food on shrinking ice shelves. Whales were hunted and killed, elephants were shot for their tusks and plastic bags were pulled from the stomachs of dead sea birds. The presenter called it the sixth mass extinction and said the planet was at the point of no return, just like the Newt had said at the rally.

It wasn't just happening overseas either. Another video explained how humans were destroying natural habitats in the UK too, with animals like hedgehogs, dormice, hares, bats and even bees now seriously under threat.

After half an hour Marty was still in tears. He thought he'd known all about the problem, but he had to admit he'd had no idea just how bad it was. Some kids from his school had taken the day off to join climate change protests a few times, but he'd never bothered. He'd kind of assumed someone else would sort it all out. Maybe he should have cared more.

But what could he do to help now? He wanted to stop the airport somehow. It was only one, small part of the problem, but everything would help wouldn't it? He wondered again whether he should tell Jumi about the meeting he'd overheard. Could they use that somehow? He still wasn't sure they could, and he was still worried that telling her would get him and his mum into big trouble.

Marty's phone interrupted his thoughts. It was another message from Jumi, asking if he wanted to meet up the next day. He didn't need to check his diary to know that he had nothing planned, so he wiped his eyes and messaged her back to say yes. She said it was supposed to be sunny again, so they should go skateboarding. He hadn't done that for ages, and was a bit worried he'd embarrass himself, but he said yes. She suggested the South Bank, which he thought he knew how to get to, so he said OK. They arranged a time to meet. Maybe he'd have decided what to do with his illegally obtained information by then.

There was a knock on the door.

'Who is it?'

'It's me,' he heard Mum say. 'Can I come in?'

'OK,' he said, giving his eyes another wipe so she wouldn't see he'd been crying.

She took a seat on the chair by his desk and looked at him with concern written all over her face.

'I've been thinking,' she began.

'About what?'

'About you. I know it's not ideal for you, living here.'

Marty nodded. She wasn't wrong.

'And I realise it was hard for you, leaving your school and your friends and having to move here. You used to be out all the time with your friends back home didn't you, and now you're cooped up in here all day.'

He nodded again. Where was she going with this?

'It's not good for you. I want to do something to help. I can't just let you come and go as you please, it just wouldn't be safe, but you should have a bit more freedom. You should be able to get out and about a bit more.'

Marty, of course, didn't mention that he could get "out and about" perfectly well now thank you very much.

'I'll have a word with Leishman. Ask him to take you out somewhere. Wherever you fancy.'

'OK,' he said cautiously.

'I know he looks scary, but he's quite friendly once you get to know him. I'll ask him to take you bowling, or to the cinema or something. I'd take you myself, but I'm going to be flat out the next couple of weeks.'

Marty smiled. The thought of Leishman in the cinema was hilarious. He'd take up about three seats, and he'd have to go in the back row or nobody behind him would be able to see a thing. Mum misunderstood his smile though.

'Does that sound good? Maybe have a look online, see what's showing at the moment.'

Marty had no intention of going to the cinema with Leishman, especially as he already had plans to go skateboarding with Jumi, but he didn't want to disappoint Mum. The thought was there he supposed.

'OK,' he said. 'I'll see if we can sort something out.'

'Great,' Mum smiled. She got up and gave her son a hug.

'I wish things weren't so difficult for you Marty,' she told him as she stepped away. 'I'll make it up to you, I promise.'

She gave him a smile as she left the room. Marty smiled to himself again. Bowling with Leishman would be just as awkward as the cinema. His fingers would never fit into the balls. Skateboarding with Jumi was definitely a better bet.

Blackmail

The next day Marty still wasn't sure whether to tell Jumi what he knew or not. He overheard Emily and Mum talking about the Cabinet meeting she had later that morning, so he decided to listen in again to see if they said anything more about the airport. That might help him make up his mind.

He sneaked into the Cabinet Office before the meeting started and set out his pencil case with the pen-bug in it and folder again. He thought maybe he should stay in there and at least pretend to do some work, just for the look of it, but then thought, no-one had seen him go in, so how would they know how long he'd been in there for? Besides, there was no way he wanted to risk bumping into Skelton again, or any of the others either to be honest. So he left his stuff on the end of the table, exactly where it had been before, and headed back to his room.

He opened his laptop and waited for the meeting to start. He didn't have long to wait before he heard someone enter the room.

'Alan,' said the unmistakably chilling voice of the Chancellor. 'I'm glad we've got the chance to talk before the meeting starts.'

‘Yes, Sir Jarvis? What did you want to discuss?’ Angry Alan replied, sounding as grumpy as he did last time Marty had heard him. Despite the fact that seemed so angry Marty had quite liked him, as he was one of the few who’d been against the airport at the meeting.

‘Alan, we simply must put all this silliness about the airport to bed, mustn’t we.’

Marty’s ears pricked up at the mention of the airport. Why were they talking about it in secret before the meeting started? That sounded dodgy. He sat up and turned the volume up so he could hear exactly what they were saying.

'Silliness? I'm not sure there's anything silly about preventing the destruction of acres of ancient woodland that's home to hundreds of different species of plants and animals, is there?'

'I'm not sure you've really grasped the issue Alan. You see, it's absolutely vital that the airport gets approved, and quickly.'

'That's what you said yesterday, but there are arguments for and against aren't there, as we discussed.'

'Arguments for and against. Yes, but much more powerful arguments for, I think one finds.'

'No, I disagree.'

'Well, perhaps I can change your mind. You see, some associates of mine stand to make an *awful* lot of money from the airport development. A ridiculous amount of money. And they're generous men and women, Alan. They're willing to share some of it, if it's worth their while. They're always on the look-out for new "consultants" who can assist them, especially "consultants" who might be able to, how can I put it, oil the wheels of government. If you'd like proof of just how generous they can be, perhaps you'd like to visit me at my new holiday home in the South of France some time.'

What was he hearing? That wasn't allowed was it? He was sure that was a word for that kind of thing. Whatever it was he was sure it wasn't right.

‘So, let me get this straight,’ said Alan. ‘You’re trying to get me to abandon my principles and to vote for the airport to be built just so that you and your friends can make a shed-load of money. And if I do, I’ll make a lot of money too.’

‘That’s essentially it, yes.’

‘A bribe, in other words.’

That was it.

‘Well, “bribe” is such an ungentlemanly term, but yes, I suppose you could call it that.’

‘You must be joking, and don’t think that I’m not going to report you for this either.’

‘Oh, I don’t think you will be doing anything of the sort. If you’re not willing to take advantage of such a generous offer you leave me no choice but to put it to you another way. Alan, as you are no doubt aware, I have a very good relationship with certain elements of the press.’

‘What, you mean your brother is editor of one national newspaper, your father owns another and it’s well-known that you’re very good friends with a man who owns two TV channels and three newspapers? You were holidaying with him on his yacht last month weren’t you?’

‘Exactly. Well done Alan, I knew you’d be on the ball with this.’

Something told Marty this was really not good.

‘OK, but, what has that got to do with the airport?’

'Oh, it has everything to do with the airport, as you're about to find out. You see, I have it on very good authority that a story might be about to hit the headlines very shortly about someone very close to you.'

'What? What are you talking about?'

'A story about a young man, shall we call him Gavin, who just might have been on the verge of being expelled from his *very* expensive school for stealing from his fellow pupils, that is until his father stepped in and had a quiet word with the headmaster and another boy took the blame and was expelled instead. Then the whole thing was forgotten about. Hushed up. Until now that is.'

Alan was angry again. In fact, he was furious.

'This is outrageous! My son wouldn't... I didn't...'

'No? Well, that really is a shame isn't it. Because the press are about to tell the world that he would, and you did.'

Alan was right, thought Marty, this was outrageous. If he understood right, Skelton was threatening to use his contacts to ruin Alan and his son. Marty had thought there was something evil about him, and he was right. Poor Angry Alan.

'You... you can't do that.'

'Well, we shall see, shan't we?'

'But, but I'll speak to the school, to the headmaster. He'll tell the truth. He'll say that it never happened.'

'Oh, one might think so mightn't one? However, one must remember that it would be disastrous for a school that relies so heavily on the generous donations of a certain individual that we might like to refer to as a media tycoon to upset said media tycoon.'

There was a long, silent pause. Marty realised he was holding his breath, waiting for one of them to speak.

'In other words,' Skelton continued with an extra edge in his voice, 'the headmaster will do *exactly* as he's told if he doesn't want to lose a quarter of his annual budget overnight. Which means, I'm quite sure, that he *will* do exactly as he's told… As, I'm also quite sure, will *you*.'

Alan let out a long sigh.

'But this would ruin me. And Gavin.'

'Oh, would it? Do you know, I think you might just be right,' sneered Skelton.

'You can't do this.'

'I think you'll find that I can. If one turns ones nose up at the carrot, one must expect to face the stick.'

Carrots? Sticks? Oiling wheels? Marty was struggling to keep up, but he thought he just about understood what was going on. Skelton had tried to bribe Alan to get him to support the airport, but as that hadn't worked he was blackmailing him instead.

'This is *totally* out of order Sir Jarvis, and highly illegal, and you know it.'

'Oh, is it? Oh dear. What a shame.'

'But… I can see that I really don't have a choice.'

‘I did so hope you might see it that way. So I can rely on your support then when we discuss the airport later?’

There was a pause, before Alan spoke again.

‘Yes,’ he said quietly. ‘You’ll have my support.’

‘Excellent,’ said Skelton, just before Marty heard the door open and general chatter started to fill the room as the other ministers arrived.

He could hardly believe what he had just heard. One minister had basically just blackmailed another to make him do what he and his dodgy mates wanted him to do. Unbelievable! He had to do something now didn’t he? But what? Who would believe him if he told anyone? And what would Skelton and his dodgy mates do to *him* if they found out he’d grassed them up?

Very bad news

'OK,' Marty heard his mum say after the general chatter had died down. 'We'll have to make this quick because some of us have a meeting with the EU Commissioner, so, no bickering today, do I make myself clear?'

There was a general mumbling of agreement. Marty was as relieved at that as his mum probably was.

'Good. So, the first item on the agenda is Winston Churchill Airport again. Has anyone got any updates for us?'

'Perhaps you've all had a chance to look at the report I emailed you last night?' asked Skelton.

'I read it this morning,' said Mum. 'It does make some very interesting points about the carbon reduction programmes the major airlines and airports are putting into place.'

'It does, doesn't it?' said Skelton smugly.

'Although, I did have a few concerns about how impartial it was,' added Mum, 'seeing as it was put together by the airlines and airports.'

'Yeah, are you for real Sir Jarvis?' said Clive. 'None of the technology it talks about as the solution to carbon emissions actually exists. It might at some point in the future, but by then it'll be too late.'

'There's always someone who stands in the way of change isn't there,' Skelton told him.
'You'd have us all going back to a time when we all travelled around on a horse and cart would you?'

'Don't be ridiculous. That's not what I'm saying, as you very well know,' Clive told him crossly.

'Alan, you were telling me just now how impressed you were with the report, weren't you?' said Skelton, with a definite edge to his voice.

'I was? Oh, yes, I was,' said Alan, who still seemed flustered from their earlier conversation. 'Yes. Very convincing.'

'Really mate?' Clive sounded shocked. 'That piece of one-sided, biased, climate-change-denying propaganda? Convincing? What are you saying?'

'We're all entitled to our own opinion Clive,' snarled Skelton.

'But not all of us have totally changed our opinion overnight. What exactly are you saying Alan?' Clive demanded.

'I'm saying,' began Alan, before pausing. 'I'm saying that I think we should go ahead with it now.'

'What!?' spluttered Clive furiously 'What's happened to you man?'

'Should we ask again how people stand on the issue Charlotte?' suggested Skelton, clearly anxious to move on, before Alan got the chance to explain what had changed his mind.

'Yes, OK,' Mum agreed. 'Alan?'

There was a short silence before he answered.

'For.'

'Clive?'

'Against.'

'Henrietta?'

'For.'

'Gurinda?'

'For.'

Oh no. She'd changed her mind as well. Marty wondered how Skelton had managed that.

'Barry?'

'For.'

'And Sir Jarvis?'

'For.'

'So, that's now five for and one against.'

This was very bad news. Skelton's plot to blackmail Alan into supporting the airport had worked, and now almost all of the Cabinet were going to vote for it. He had to do something, but he still had no idea what.

'And you, Charlotte?' asked Skelton.

'I'm still not sure.'

'But Charlotte, it's almost unanimous now.'

'Almost, but not quite Sir Jarvis. I think we should all spend the next few days giving this *careful* consideration, doing as much independent research as we can and finding out what the public thinks. Don't forget, some people feel very strongly about this, and not just the protesters.'

Skelton started to complain, but Mum cut him short.

'I think that will do for today. I'm sure we all have things we need to be doing.'

Marty heard the sound of them gathering their papers up and one-by-one leaving the room.

He waited until the coast was clear, then sneaked back down to the Cabinet Office to collect his gear. Just as he reached for the door handle to get back out the door swung open, making him jump. Leishman stood in the doorway, blocking his escape. He looked angry, although to be fair, he always looked angry.

He looked down at Marty and said 'I think you and me need to have a little chat, don't we?'

Caught red-handed

Marty didn't particularly want a chat with Leishman to be honest, but he didn't really think he had much of a choice. The big security guard closed the door behind him without taking his eyes off Marty.

'Care to tell me what's going on here?' he demanded.

'I've just been doing homework,' Marty told him. 'I got interrupted when the meeting started, so I've just come back to get my stuff.'

'Ah, doing your homework? I see. Get much done did you?'

Marty was hoping he wouldn't be asked that.

'Um, not loads. I was just getting started.'

'But some though?'

'Well, yeah.'

'What subject was it you were doing?'

What had he been doing?

'Um, history.'

'"Um history" eh? Not sure I studied "um history" at school.'

Marty laughed nervously. Leishman didn't.

'So, let's have a look at the "not loads" of "um history" you've done then.'

Marty didn't move. He knew there was nothing in his folder he could show him. He was pretty sure Leishman knew that as well.

'Come on Marty, don't be shy,' he prompted. 'What have you been learning about?'

He wracked his brains for something history-related.

'Prime Ministers,' he blurted out.

'Go on then. Tell me what Prime Ministers you've been learning about.'

He tried his best to remember some of the names Leishman had mentioned the other day.

'Um, Tadpole, Boy-George, Pitt the Dumb and Dumber, Gladiator and The Duke… of… Wonderland?'

Leishman just raised a questioning eyebrow at him.

'OK, you're right. I haven't really been doing any history. I have got a load of stuff I'm supposed to be doing but I haven't even looked at it yet.'

'Oh, I see,' he said, pursing his lips. 'Well, that won't do will it. You'll be in trouble when you get back to school if you don't get it done won't you.'

Marty nodded.

'I remember when I was at school, if you didn't do your homework you had a choice. You could either be chained to a radiator in the cellar for a week, clean the hall floor with your tongue or clear all the dog mess off the football pitches with your bare hands.'

'What?!' Marty almost shouted. 'That can't be allowed.'

Leishman actually smiled. 'Got you. Of course we didn't have to do those things. I always did my homework anyway, as I'm sure you will at some time between now and the end of the holidays. But, what really interests me right now, is why you keep coming in here *pretending* to do homework. What's really going on Marty?'

For a second Marty thought about playing Leishman at his own game and making up something completely ridiculous in the hope that he bought it, but he was pretty sure he wouldn't fall for it, and he couldn't think of anything on the spot anyway. He was going to have to tell him the truth, although, there was a fair chance he wouldn't believe that either.

'You're right,' he admitted. 'I haven't been doing homework.'

Leishman nodded.

'I didn't think there was any chance a boy your age would get his homework done at the *start* of the holidays. If you only had one day left before it had to be handed in I might just have believed you.'

Marty kicked himself. He should have thought of that.

'So, what I've actually been doing is…' He took a deep breath, '…spying on Cabinet meetings.'

He waited for a reaction. Leishman didn't blow his top immediately, which he took to be a good sign.

'Spying on Cabinet meetings?'

He nodded.

'Why on *earth* would you want to do that?'

Leishman seemed more concerned by Marty's sanity than the possible breach of national security, which he took as a good sign.

‘Well, the first time it was an accident,’ he explained. ‘You see, I actually *was* thinking about doing some homework, I was so bored, but my room was being cleaned, so I came in here, but I got interrupted, and I left my pencil case in here when I left, which had a listening-bug-pen in it, and I wanted to know when the meeting finished, so I listened in, and I heard them talking about the airport plans, and Jumi, she’s this girl I met when I went out of the secret passage, thanks for telling me about that by the way, she’d told me all about the damage the airport will do and climate change and everything, so I decided to listen to the next meeting, which was today.’

He stopped to catch his breath. Leishman looked like he was still trying to take that all in.

‘OK,’ he said. ‘Is that all?’

‘Yes,’ said Marty, but Leishman could clearly see that it wasn’t. ‘Well. No.’

‘Go on.’

He wasn’t sure whether to tell Leishman what he’d heard Skelton saying, but he was sure that he’d know he was lying if he tried to make anything up.

'Well. Just now, before the meeting, I heard that Sir Jarvis Skelton talking to one of the others, I don't know his full name, Alan something, one of the other ministers. Anyway, Skelton told him that if he didn't support the new airport then he'd get the papers to print a story about his son being caught stealing at school, and the only reason he hadn't been expelled was because Alan had sorted it with the headmaster.'

Leishman thought about this for a while.

'Blackmail?'

'Yeah, and he offered him money too if he pretended to be a consultant for them. And it worked as well. Alan was dead against the airport yesterday but voted for it today.'

He thought about it some more.

'Well, that really is very serious.'

Marty nodded again.

'What are you going to do about it?' he asked.

'*Me*? What am *I* going to do about it?'

It was Leishman's turn to nod.

'Can't *you* do something about it?'

'I can hardly do anything can I? I'm supposed to be maintaining security, not helping twelve-year-old boys spy on the Government.'

'Yeah, but… something needs to be done.'

'Yes, I think it does. Which is why I'm sure you'll think of something.'

Marty puffed out his cheeks.

'I'm not sure I will.'

Leishman walked over to the window and looked outside. It wasn't raining today, but it wasn't very sunny either at the moment.

'I know Chumley Woods well,' he said, still looking out of the window. 'I grew up near there. Used to walk my dog in the woods there, play with my friends in the fields, dam the streams, climb trees. It's beautiful there. And full of wildlife. We used to see rabbits, hedgehogs, badgers, foxes, even deer sometimes.'

Any gorillas? Marty wondered.

'And loads of birds. Owls, kestrels, woodpeckers, cuckoos, kingfishers, mistle thrushes. I fell in love with the birds. Such graceful creatures, sweeping and swooping, hanging in the wind. Not to mention their beautiful songs. That's why I still go birdwatching there.'

Marty thought he was joking again.

'Yeah, OK.'

'No,' Leishman insisted, turning back round. 'I really do go bird-watching there. I'm not having you on.'

'Oh,' said Marty.

'You'll have to come with me sometime.'

Marty tried to picture him, with binoculars and a camera, tiptoeing through the woods to get a glimpse of a bristle brush or whatever it was called. He struggled, to be honest.

'So I really, *really* don't want this airport to be built.'

'I see.'

'Especially if some jumped up snob with rich, powerful friends is going to bully everyone into agreeing to build it just so he can stick a few million more pounds in his offshore bank account.'

'No.'

'So you've got to stop him Marty. You've got to find a way to stop him.'

'Right.'

'I'm trusting you Marty. Don't let me down.'

He held Marty's gaze as he marched past him and out of the room.

Marty waited for a minute, not sure how to react. Now Leishman was expecting him to do something save the woods, as Jumi would if she knew what he knew. Life was so much easier when he was bored.

He still had no idea what he could do without landing himself in trouble, but people were starting to rely on him now. He didn't like it. It was too stressful, too much responsibility. Why did he ever want to be an eco warrior?

On the plus side, at least Leishman hadn't asked Marty if he wanted to go to cinema with him.

He was about to get his stuff when he thought, he may as well leave it there. If Leishman didn't mind it being there, and Mum and her colleagues didn't seem to even notice it, it was easier to keep it there. So he did.

He wondered what else he was going to hear.

The stench of a thousand backsides

Marty knew what he was doing this time. He waited for an empty lift, pressed 1 and 0 together, walked through the little room under the house and through the big door into the passage. He had his pen-torch ready, and was soon in the little room at the other end. The lift arrived quickly, and before he knew it, he was leaving the station.

He crossed Westminster Bridge then headed past the London Eye and onto the South Bank, past all sorts of street entertainers: break-dancers, a man making giant bubbles, musicians and a magician. He stopped briefly to look at some human statues - a golden lady, a Grim Reaper and a Yoda who looked like he was floating in mid-air (how do they do that?) – but then Big Ben started to chime behind him and he realised he was late, and he hurried on towards the skate park.

Actually, it wasn't officially a skate-park. It was a space under some big building on the South Bank of the Thames. It was perfect for skateboarding though, with ramps and grind rails, all surrounded by some pretty cool graffiti. Jumi was waiting for him when he got there. She had an orange t-shirt with the Eco Now logo on it today. Marty wondered how many different colours she had it in.

'Sorry I'm late,' he told her.

'It's fine,' she said. 'Come on.'

She dropped her board down and flew down a ramp. Marty did the same and followed her. He'd brought his old board, not the fancy-pants, expensive one he'd been given by the UK champion when she'd visited Downing Street. It was a bit battered, but he thought that using the new one would have led to too many questions he didn't want to answer.

He was a bit rusty, as he hadn't been able to get out much for a few months since they'd moved into Number 10, but he soon got back into it. Jumi was good, but Marty didn't embarrass himself, and he managed not to suffer any injuries, which would have made going back home more than a bit awkward.

After about half an hour they took a break and sat down on a low wall at the side.

'So, did you look at that stuff I sent you?' Jumi asked him, picking up her board.

Marty took his off too and put it on the wall next to him.

'Yeah. It's scary isn't it.'

'Just a bit.'

'I couldn't believe just how much is under threat. It's terrible. And it's only going to get worse unless we do something now. It's good some of you are trying to do something about it.'

'Nothing's going to change if we keep building new airports though,' she said.

'Do you think it can be stopped?' he asked, thinking about what he'd heard that morning and the day before.

'Of course,' she answered, 'if we can get those idiot politicians to care about something other than their own careers for once. The more people we can get out onto the streets to tell them what we think the better.'

'Yeah,' he said. 'Well, tell me when the next rally is and I'll be there.'

'Cool.'

Marty felt guilty, knowing that he had information that could be vital in helping to stop the airport. Really though, what could they do with it? Who would believe him, and would it make any difference if they did?

'I just wish there was something more we could do,' said Jumi, as if reading his mind.

'I know,' he agreed. 'Maybe we'll think of something.'

She didn't answer him. They sat and watched the other skateboarders for a while.

'Do you fancy an ice-cream?' Marty asked after a bit, remembering she'd said she liked it.

'Sure.'

They picked up their boards and walked over to a nearby ice-cream van. They joined the long queue behind a load of tourists who were happily enjoying their day-out without the weight of worrying about the planet on their shoulders. Marty wished he could feel that way again. They eventually reached the front and bought a couple of 99s, with raspberry sauce, then sat on a nearby bench to eat them.

'Are your parents working today?' Jumi suddenly asked.

'It's just my Mum,' he told her, 'but she's working, yeah.'

'What does she do?'

He wasn't sure how to answer that. He still didn't want her to know who he was, especially after what she'd just said about politicians, in case she didn't want to be his friend any more.

'Oh, just some boring job in an office,' he said, which was kind of true, if you didn't mention where exactly her office was. 'How about you?'

'It's just me and my Dad. He does some freelance work sometimes, whatever that means, but he spends most of his time doing Eco Now stuff.'

They ate in silence for a while. Marty was being careful to avoid any tell-tale raspberry sauce drips down his chin this time, both to avoid suspicion from Emily when he got home and as it would have been pretty embarrassing to dribble down his chin both times he'd met his new friend.

'You're pretty good,' he told her after a while, pointing at her board.

'Thanks,' she said. 'You're not too bad either.'

'I don't get to do it much these days,' he said, then immediately regretted it.

'Why's that?' she asked.

'Oh, um, since we moved house, we're not near anywhere good, and Mum's not keen on me going out on my own,' he managed.

Fortunately she didn't ask him where he lived.

'Did you have to move schools?'

'Yeah. I hate it. It's full of losers.'

'So's mine.'

'One or two of them are OK, but most of them treat me like I'm some kind of freak, just because I'm not like them.'

'Like what?'

'Rich. Stuck up. You know.'

'Yeah.'

'My mates back home, they were just normal. Nobody at my new school is just normal. Apart from Jamie Tancock, he's quite normal I suppose. He's OK. When he's not in the toilet.'

'What?'

'Nothing. Doesn't matter. So what's yours like?'

'My toilet?'

'No, your school.'

'Oh. It's OK. Not good, not bad. Just, OK.'

'I bet my teachers are worse than yours.'

'Bet they're not.'

'Bet they are. In my school the teachers give you detention for a week if they see you with your shirt untucked.'

'Well in my school they ban you from the prom if you forget your journal just once.'

Marty wasn't going to be outdone. He knew his school was *definitely* the worst in the world.

'OK, but in my school they make sure you're last to go in for lunch if you're even a second late for school, so all that's left is the lumpiest, coldest, greasiest, grim sludge in the tray, that everyone knows the dinner ladies have just scraped up off the floor.'

'In my school, if your skirt is just one centimetre too short, they make you change into the stinkiest, skankiest pair of lime green joggers they can find in the lost property box, with stains that you really don't want to know where they came from and the stench of a thousand backsides.'

He didn't think he could top that, but then he remembered something that Leishman had told him that he thought he could use.

'Yeah, well if we don't do our homework you get the choice of getting chained to the football pitch, cleaning the radiators with dog mess or licking your tongue with your hands.'

Jumi frowned at him like he was completely mad. It had sounded better when Leishman had said it, he had to admit.

'What?'

'Well, something like that anyway.' It was time to change the subject. 'So, have you got many friends?'

'Not really. Everyone just thinks I'm the weird eco warrior girl.'

'That figures.'

'Oi!'

'Joke. There's nothing wrong with being an eco warrior anyway. I reckon I'm going to make a good eco warrior.'

That made her laugh.

'You've only been to one rally so far.' Marty's face fell, but she noticed straight away and added, 'But stick with it. We can make an eco warrior of you yet.'

That was what he wanted to hear.

'Have you got a nickname, at school?' she asked, before taking another bite of her 99.

'No. Well, not that I know of. My sister has one for me though.'

'What is it?'

'I'm not telling you.'

'Go on. I'll tell you mine if you tell me yours.'

'Promise?'

'Promise.'

'Well, OK than. She thinks it's hilarious to call me Marty Farty.'

He waited for her to laugh, but she didn't.

'That's pretty lame.'

'I'm glad you think so. So, go on then. What's yours?'

A smile spread across her face.

'Not telling you.'

'But you promised.'

'With my fingers crossed.'

'What does that even mean? Why does everyone think that means they can lie just because they've got their fingers crossed?'

'Dunno. I'll tell you what it is some day.'

'Promise?'

She nodded, but then held up her still-crossed fingers, then popped the last of her cone into her mouth.

‘Come on, you’d better make the most of it while you can,’ she told him, picked up her stuff and started running back to the skate-park. Marty grabbed his gear and followed her.

Twenty minutes later, still with no major injuries to either of them, Jumi looked at her watch.

‘I really should be going,’ she said. ‘Dad’ll be wondering where I am.’

‘OK,’ said Marty. ‘Do you fancy doing this again some time?’

‘Sure. I know a few other good places I can show you, new boy.’

‘Cool. Well, I’ll message you when I can get out next then.’

‘OK.’

‘OK. See you then.’

‘See you.’

They both headed home in opposite directions. Marty realised he didn’t know where Jumi lived either. As he walked back he thought more about the airport and what he’d heard the ministers talking about as he walked back to the station. He just couldn’t get it off his mind.

As he scanned his Oyster card again at the barrier he felt guilty that he hadn’t told her who he was, or what he knew. If he told her what he knew though he’d have to tell her how he knew it, and he was sure she wouldn’t want to be friends with the Prime Minister’s son, even if he had helped.

Perhaps it wasn't Jumi he should be telling anyway. Maybe he should tell his mum. Would she believe him though, and would she do anything? Or he could contact a reporter, if he could find one that wasn't working for Skelton's mates. But why would they take his word for it, and if they did would it end up with Mum losing her job, which he really didn't want, even if it would mean not having to live in Downing Street any more?

He found the right lift this time, and didn't have to wait too long to get it to himself. Soon he was back through the passage and going up in the lift at the other end. He checked there was no-one in the corridor to see him with his board, and quickly stashed them back in his room.

Just as he did his phone pinged. It was Jumi, telling him that the next rally was planned for two days' time, at midday, on Oxford Street. He messaged her straight back to tell her he'd be there. He couldn't wait.

Unbelievable

The following morning Marty got up late. Maybe he was tired from all that skateboarding. When he did get up he wandered along to the kitchen for his morning Coco-Pops. He had thought about cooking himself something for a change, like a fried egg sandwich, but he'd kind of gone off cooked breakfasts after his mum had tried to make him one a couple of weeks ago. He could almost taste the slimy egg and charcoal-coated bacon just thinking about it.

He thought about going out, maybe to the South Bank again, even if he would be on his own, but it wouldn't have been so much fun. With nothing better to do he opened up his laptop and found himself wondering whether there were any Cabinet meetings today. Perhaps he was getting into this politics thing after all. What was happening to him?

Someone was already talking when he got into the listening app, and he was glad he'd left his stuff in the office overnight, or he'd have missed it.

'Apparently the protests are going to be even bigger tomorrow Sir Jarvis,' a voice he recognised as Bald Barry was saying. 'They're hoping to get some celebrities to go along as well. They're going to be all over the news and social media, it's not going to help our cause at all.'

Celebrities? Jumi hadn't mentioned them. He wondered whether it would be anyone he recognised. Hopefully it wouldn't be anyone he'd met here at Number 10 who would recognise *him*.

'Don't worry Barry, I've still got a few tricks up my sleeve,' Skelton tried to reassure him. 'It will all be fine. I'm taking care of it.' Just the sound of his voice sent a chill down Marty's spine.

'But how?' Barry asked him. 'What can you possibly do?'

'My dear Barry, you underestimate me again. You're forgetting that I have friends in all sorts of high places. It's really very simple. All we have to do is to make sure there's a larger than usual police presence at the rally. Alan can speak to them and suggest that they equip themselves with riot gear, that's his department. Then when the violence erupts…'

'…*If* it erupts. We don't know that it will be a violent protest. The last one wasn't.'

'Oh, it will erupt all right. I've seen to that.'

This did *not* sound good.

'Have you?' asked Barry. 'How?'

'Let's just say that one or two of the "protesters" may not be there for quite the same reasons as most of those ignorant, unwashed hippies.'

'What do you mean?'

'Oh, for heaven's sake man, do I have to spell it out for you? I mean that one's business associates have paid some thugs to go along and *pretend* they're protesters, when in fact at a given signal they'll start throwing things and smashing windows and generally, I believe one could possible describe it as, *rioting*.'

For the second time in a matter of days, Marty couldn't believe what he was hearing. Yesterday Skelton was blackmailing a fellow minister into supporting his schemes, today he was planning to start a riot just so he could make the protesters look bad. Marty felt sick.

'Oh, right. I get it. Very clever, yes.'

'And of course, the police, equipped in their riot gear, will have to move in to deal with the trouble. At which point it's inevitable that more and more people will get caught up in the riot, a great many of them will end up getting arrested, and it will look terrible for them on the news.'

'But, what if the press takes the protesters' side, and starts accusing the police of being heavy-handed? Then they'll start blaming us for not managing the situation better.'

'Oh, I really don't think the press will do that, do you?' said Skelton smugly.

Barry took a second to think about that.

'Ohhh! I see. Your friends in high places again.'

'Ah, so you do have a few brain-cells inside that bald head of yours after all. Yes, it really is *very* useful to have almost all the papers and television stations on your side. And they are always so *very* grateful to be told where and when a major news story is about to break.'

'Clever, Sir Jarvis. Very clever. That'll put the protesters out of the picture, then we just need to convince the PM that she doesn't need to worry about climate change, win the vote, and it'll be full steam ahead for the airport.'

'All this climate change nonsense is a load of old guff and the sooner we all accept that the better. Never mind. I'm sure Charlotte will see the light before too long. One way or another.'

This was unbelievable. He was actually going to start a riot, blame it on innocent people and make sure the press made it look like the protesters were in the wrong and should be ignored. Innocent people could end up in prison, like Jumi's dad, or even Jumi. Skelton was pure evil. Marty couldn't let it happen. But what could he do to stop it? He was going to have to tell his mum what was going on, but somehow without letting on what he'd been doing.

Disaster

Marty heard someone coming upstairs, and shortly afterwards he recognised Mum and Emily's almost identical voices coming from the kitchen. He closed his laptop and went to see them. They were chatting about some political opinion polls or something as they made themselves sandwiches. This was his opportunity to finally say something, although he'd have to be careful not to let slip that he'd been spying on their meetings.

'Mum, can I talk to you?' he asked.

'Of course you can, although you'll have to be quick. I'm being picked up in ten minutes to go over to the Commons for Prime Minister's Questions,' said Mum.

'It's about the airport.'

'Winston Churchill Airport?'

'Yeah.'

'What about it?' she asked, taking a bite of her sandwich – cheese and pickle by the look of it. Her speciality. Even she couldn't mess those up.

'Well, are you sure it's a good idea?'

'No, I'm not sure at the moment. We're waiting for a bit more evidence about it. Why the sudden interest?'

'Oh, I was just reading some stuff about it, and about the damage we're doing to the planet.'

‘And suddenly you’re an expert,’ said Emily sarcastically.

‘I’m not saying I’m an expert, but it is going to destroy a massive amount of natural habitat, not to mention the increased carbon emissions.’

‘Listen to you,’ sneered Emily. ‘Going to the next Eco Now rally are you?’

That got his attention. Did she know what he’d been doing?

‘What?’ he asked her.

‘You’re talking like a climate protester. If you carry on like this I reckon you’ll be out there with them, waving flags and singing songs and refusing to wash and stuff.’

‘Refusing to wash?’

‘Yeah, they’re all a bit stinky aren’t they?’

‘No, they’re not.’

‘How do you know? Have you ever met one?’

‘No, of course not,’ he lied.

‘Then shut up about stuff you know nothing about.’

‘Don’t tell me to shut up.’

‘Both of you, shut up,’ Mum told them impatiently. ‘This is exactly what I don’t need right now.’

Marty was quite glad she’d stopped them actually. He was in danger of giving something away.

They ate their sandwiches in silence for a bit, while Marty got himself a packet of cheese-and-onion crisps and some orangeade. Mum was studying some papers, presumably in preparation for her meeting. After a while he decided to try again.

'Mum?'

She looked up from her papers, looking slightly irritated.

'Yes Marty.'

'Talking about the protesters, is what they're doing against the law?'

She looked at Marty carefully, and for a second he worried that she'd worked out he knew more than he was letting on.

'No. Everyone has a right to peaceful protest in this country.'

'OK, but, what if things got out of hand?'

'What do you mean?'

Now she was really looking at him questioningly, as was Emily.

'Well, what if people started fighting, or throwing things, or causing damage?'

'That would be against the law, yes,' said Mum.

'Why?' Emily asked him.

He ignored Emily and asked Mum, 'So what would the police do?'

'They'd arrest whoever was doing it. Why are you asking me this?'

'I just wondered, that's all.'

Marty wasn't sure she believed him, but she just gave him a funny look, took a bite of her sandwich and went back to her papers. He gave it a minute, then asked, 'But what if it wasn't their fault? What if someone else was causing the trouble on purpose, just to make the protesters look bad, and the police were told to expect trouble so it looked a whole lot worse than it was too?'

Mum put her papers down and really looked puzzled now, and Emily was frowning at him.

'Marty, what are you talking about?'

'I just… I was reading something about that kind of thing happening somewhere, I can't remember where. I was just worried that it could happen here too.'

'You're being ridiculous, I'm sure that sort of thing would never happen in this country.'

'Are you sure though? What if someone was organising it all, just to make it look like a riot rather than a protest?'

'I've had enough of this Marty. I don't know what you've been reading but it needs to stop. You're getting all sorts of ridiculous ideas into your head. I don't want to hear that sort of thing again, do you understand? I've really got to go now.'

She stashed her papers back in her briefcase and topped up her water bottle from the tap. Marty was pleased that she always used a refillable one and not disposable plastic, now he cared about that sort of thing. Emily was looking at him with a scornful look on her face.

'You're such an idiot Marty. Been reading conspiracy theories have you? Think the Earth is flat and the moon landing was fake do you?'

'Shut up Emily. You're the idiot.'

'Don't call me an idiot.'

'You are an idiot. Who do you think you are anyway? Always watching the news and talking about politics. You think you know it all don't you. There's something wrong with you if you're interested in politics at your age. Freak!'

'Marty!' shouted Mum. 'You do not call your sister a freak.'

'She called me an idiot.'

'You called me an idiot too,' argued Emily.

'You called me an idiot first, you freak!' he shouted back, slamming his glass down on the worktop.

'That's enough Marty!' yelled Mum. 'I've had enough of your attitude. I don't know what's wrong with you at the moment.'

'What's wrong with *me*? Why are you always taking her side?'

'I do not always take her side.'

'Yes you do. Just because she loves your stupid politics as much as you do. You never tell her off, only me. It's not fair. Stupid politics. Stupid politicians. You're all freaks!'

'That's it! I'm not having that. You need to learn how to behave yourself young man. You can't keep hurling insults at people and expect to get away with it.'

'No? That's exactly what you politicians do though isn't it.'

'That's different.'

'How is it? How is it different? It's exactly the same. You're just a bunch of idiots who're rude to each other for a living. If you can do it, so can I.'

'That's enough! You're grounded!'

'I'm a prisoner here anyway! What difference does that make?'

‘Then I’m taking your phone and laptop away.’

‘What?! That’s not fair. For how long?’

‘For as long as I say. Go and get them now.’

‘But Mum…’

‘*Now.*’

He could see from the look on her face that she meant it. Emily was smirking at him, and he was going to say something, but he didn’t want to make things even worse. He slapped his phone on the table and marched off to get his laptop. It wasn’t until he’d handed it over that he realised – he hadn’t warned Jumi about Skelton’s plan, and he wouldn’t be able to now unless he got his phone or laptop back.

‘Can’t I keep my phone at least?’ he pleaded.

‘No. You can have them back when you’ve learnt to control yourself,’ she told him firmly. ‘And don’t even think about asking security if you can go out. They’ll be under strict instructions that you’re grounded - you’re not to go anywhere.’

Marty thought about questioning whether grounding the children of the Prime Minister was really what security were supposed to be worrying about, but thought better of it. Mum picked up her briefcase.

‘See you later,’ she said coldly, and left, taking Marty’s phone and laptop with her.

This was a disaster, and it was all Marty’s fault. He had to find a way to sort it.

The riot

That afternoon was the longest and most frustrating of Marty's life. He spent most of it in his bedroom. He was desperate to contact Jumi to warn her about what was going to happen at the rally, and unable to find anything remotely interesting to do. He tried reading a few of his books, but he couldn't get into any of them. He even thought about reading the book about the US President, but he wasn't quite that desperate.

Mum had left Marty and Emily a note telling them to microwave a frozen shepherd's pie each, and they sat and ate it without speaking or even looking at each other. Mum was out at some meeting or other, still with Marty's phone and laptop. With nothing better to do he went to bed early and watched rubbish TV until he fell asleep.

* * *

Mum had already left by the time he got up for breakfast the next morning, but she had left him a note saying that he could have his devices back at the end of the day if he behaved himself. If he behaved himself? How old did she think he was? That would be too late anyway, the rally was at midday.

With Mum out of the way, and no sign of Emily, he made a decision. He was going to sneak out and warn Jumi and everyone else there. He didn't know if they'd believe him, but maybe Jumi could speak to her dad and he could let people know.

He quickly made himself some ketchup on toast as they were out of milk, ate it as quickly as he could, jumped in and out of the shower and got dressed. He grabbed his torch-pen and cap (he didn't think he needed the sunglasses disguise any more), and went downstairs towards the lift. It was busy though, with people constantly coming and going. He hung around impatiently, waiting for his chance. Everyone was too busy to notice him fortunately.

Finally, the lift became free. He ran towards it and got in just as the doors started to close. When they closed behind him he pressed 1 and 0, and took a deep breath as the lift went down, thinking about what he was about to do and the trouble he could be getting himself into.

When he got out of the lift at Westminster station, instead of going through the barrier and outside he quickly found a tube map on the wall to work out where he needed to go. He'd been to Oxford Street on a family shopping trip once (four hours of utter boredom whilst Mum and Emily tried on clothes), and he was pretty sure that he needed Oxford Circus station. He found it on the map and worked out the quickest way to get there. He ran to the Jubilee Line platform, and only had to wait a couple of minutes for a train.

When one arrived it was rammed, and he had to squeeze on to find a place to stand, trying to breathe as little as possible as he found himself crushed up against a man who smelled like his idea of good personal hygiene was having a bath once a year and using deodorant, well, never. Fortunately, Marty was only going one stop, and he fought his way off the train at Green Park and took a deep breath of slightly fresher air as he jumped down onto the platform.

Marty spotted the sign for the Victoria Line, and started running, weaving his way in and out of business people, families and groups of tourists. He ran along hot, stuffy corridors, up escalators and down stairs. It was a long way from one platform to the other, through a maze of corridors, but he eventually got there, out of breath and a bit sweaty, just as a train left the station. He got his breath back as he waited for the next one.

He didn't have to wait long, and he was relieved to see that it was much quieter than the last one as it screeched to a stop. He jumped on and even got a seat this time. Soon he was hopping off again, at Oxford Circus, and he ran through the crowds, bumping into shopping bags and hurdling a sausage dog as he went. He found the exit, swiped his card, and ran out onto Oxford Street.

It only took a couple of seconds for him to realise that he was too late. The Eco Now protesters were to his right, as colourful and noisy as last time, but on his left was a line of police officers behind a row of riot shields. Someone was shouting at the protesters through a megaphone, telling them to leave. Shoppers were hurrying away as quickly as they could, and Marty could see some of the shops trying to close up and pulling the metal grilles down in front of their windows. It was very different to the Trafalgar Square rally, where everyone had seemed happy and the police had been laughing and joking with the protesters.

He started walking towards the protesters, wondering if he should really be heading back home instead. There were film crews, reporters and photographers everywhere, as Skelton had planned, and overhead he could hear helicopters hovering, presumably belonging to the police or TV stations or both.

He reached the crowd, but it felt really weird. It was as if everyone could feel that something bad was about to happen. One or two people were leaving, but most of them seemed to be standing firm. He made his way through the people, desperately looking for Jumi. He saw Art, who wasn't cooking burgers or dancing today, then the man who had been addressing the crowd in Trafalgar Square, The Newt, deep in conversation with some other men and women. They all looked very concerned. He heard a noise behind him and looked around to see some armoured cars arriving behind the line of police. He wanted to go and warn The Newt what Skelton was trying to make happen, that they needed to keep calm and not give the police any reason to move in, but before he could get to him he suddenly melted away into the crowd.

He started looking for Jumi again, and finally spotted her at the edge of the throng. He fought his way through to her.

'You made it,' she said when she saw her friend approaching.

'Only just.'

'Something's wrong,' she said.

'I know. I think something bad's about to happen.'

'I don't understand. Why are all those police here? They never send that many police along. Why are they here now?'

Marty knew the answer to that, but didn't let on. There wasn't any point in telling her now, and it would only give away who he was.

'They're just waiting for an excuse to start arresting people,' he said.

Jumi gave him a puzzled look.

'That's what I reckon, anyway,' he added quickly.

'But nobody's going to do anything that bad,' she said. 'We never do.'

At that exact moment she was proved wrong though. There was an earth-shattering crash that made them both jump, followed by the tinkling of falling glass. Someone had hurled a metal bin through a shop window.

'What's happening?' shouted Jumi over the screams and shouts that followed.

A fight broke out at the back of the crowd, and seconds later another window was smashed. The police had seen enough. With the visors down on their black helmets and their batons out they started to advance, a wall of ominous shields marching towards Marty, Jumi and the others. Some of the protesters started shouting back, and started to link arms to form a line across the road, and someone threw a milkshake towards the police, which just splatted in the road in front of them. For some reason Marty found himself hoping that none of those celebrities had turned up to support them.

'Come on,' he told Jumi. 'We really need to get out of here.'

Jumi just stood though, rooted to the spot, staring in disbelief at the scene unfolding around her. Marty noticed the photographers and cameramen having a field day. There was even a drone hovering overhead now, trying to get the best pictures.

'I don't understand,' she said again.

'Jumi,' he told her. 'It's not safe here. We need to get out of here.'

Another window was broken, and the shouting got louder and louder. The few remaining shoppers fled in panic. More drinks were being thrown at the police, but they just swatted them away with their shields. They were getting closer and closer to the protesters in front of the two friends. It was starting to get really scary.

'Come on,' Marty pleaded.

'My dad,' she said though. 'I don't know where my dad is.'

'I'm sure he's OK,' Marty tried to reassure her. 'He wouldn't want you here would he, right in the middle of this.'

She seemed in two minds.

'He'll be fine. We need to go,' he told her.

He grabbed her hand, and together they started running from the battleground, dodging the broken glass and the fights. Another line of police had appeared behind them, trying to block the protesters in, but they spotted a gap at the edge and sprinted towards it. Jumi gave one look back over her shoulder, looking for her dad, as they made it past the second line of police. Then they just ran.

They ran and ran, away from Oxford Street and onto Regent Street. They slowed down a bit as the noise faded behind them, but kept on going. They finally stopped for breath at Piccadilly Circus, and sat down on some steps. It was weird to see everyone going about their business as if nothing had happened, so close to what they'd just seen. Jumi looked pale, and she anxiously looked back towards where they'd just come from. They could still hear the sounds of shouting and sirens in the distance.

'I don't get it,' she said, shaking her head. 'We've never had trouble before. Not like that. Why would anyone start breaking windows and fighting now?'

'They're not real protesters,' Marty answered, without thinking. She looked at him with a frown.

'What?'

He couldn't not tell her now.

'The people causing trouble, they're not real Eco Now supporters. They were there just to make trouble. To make Eco Now look bad. To give the police an excuse to arrest people.'

She carried on frowning at him.

'You might be right.' She paused. 'You said that like you knew it was true though, not like you were guessing.'

'Did I?'

'Yes. You did. What do you know about this Marty? There's never been any violence before, then you turn up and suddenly this happens. What's going on Marty?'

It was time to come clean.

The truth

'It's nothing to do with me,' Marty told Jumi, 'but I did overhear something. Some politicians planned all this today. They planted people in the crowd to cause trouble, made sure the police were expecting a riot and told the news reporters to be here to see it all. I wanted to warn you but my Mum confiscated my phone and laptop.'

She looked stunned.

'Marty, how would you know all that?'

He took a deep breath.

'Jumi, I haven't been entirely truthful with you.'

Jumi looked at him with disgust, jumped up and started walking away.

'No, it's not what you think,' he protested, following her.

'Keep away from me Marty,' she told him. 'I don't know what you've done but I can't trust you anymore. You've lied to me.'

'Jumi, listen to me. I've done nothing wrong. I just, I just get to hear things sometimes, at home.'

She stopped and turned to face him.

'What are you talking about?'

'It's my mum.'

'What about your mum?'

'My mum. I told you she did a boring office job. She's actually the Prime Minister. I live in 10 Downing Street. I overheard something yesterday where one of her ministers came up with this plan. Like I said, I was going to warn you but I couldn't.'

Jumi didn't seem to know what to make of that.

'Take your cap off,' she told him, so he did.

'You do look a bit familiar,' she said.

'It's all true,' he insisted.

'Your mum's the Prime Minister. Charlotte Marsh. Wow. Did *she* know this was going to happen today?'

'No. Some of the other MPs set it up. They're working with these rich and powerful businessmen and newspaper owners. It wasn't her fault.'

'How exactly do you know this? I assume they don't invite you along to their meetings.'

'You probably wouldn't believe me.'

'Try me.'

'OK, so, I was given this secret service pen, which isn't really a pen, it's a listening device, and I left it in the room where they have their meetings, and I can hear everything they say on my laptop.'

'You're right, I don't believe you,' she said. 'Actually,' she added, 'I think I do. I can't think of another way you'd know all that. Assuming you're telling the truth.'

'I am.'

'OK. So, didn't you tell your mum this was going to happen?'

'I tried, but she didn't listen.'

'Brilliant.'

She started walking again, slowly, back towards Oxford Street.

'You should have told me the truth Marty. Did you think I wouldn't like you, just because of who your mum was?'

'Well, yeah, I suppose so.'

She just looked at him and shook her head. He knew he'd upset her.

'So, what now?' he asked.

She looked thoughtful, then she stopped, and a smile slowly spread across her face.

'Marty, your mum's the Prime Minister.'

'Well, yes?'

'Think about it. She's in charge of the country. She can stop the airport, she can cut our carbon emissions to zero, she can stop everything being destroyed, and she can tell the rest of the world to do the same!'

'Um, I'm not sure it's that simple.'

'Of course it is. You've just got to persuade her Marty.'

'Me?'

Why did everyone think he was capable of doing anything remotely useful? First Leishman, now Jumi.

'Yes, you. She's your mum.'

'Yeah, but she never listens to anything I've got to say.'

'Show her those videos I sent you. Tell her all about it. The Earth's dying Marty. It's up to you to make her understand that.'

'Yeah, but…'

‘It’s the point of no return *now*. Soon it’ll be too late to do anything. You’ve *got* to convince her. You can’t let those dodgy politicians get away with it.’

This sounded huge. Marty wasn’t ready to be at the middle of all that. What if it all went wrong?

‘I’m not sure,’ he said. ‘I don’t know whether she’ll believe me, and I’d have to tell her I’ve been spying on her meetings which will get me into a massive load of trouble. It’s got to be against the law. And I don’t know what it would do to her career either.’

‘Marty, the planet is dying, and you’re worried about getting into trouble and your mum’s career?’

‘Well, yes, I guess.’

‘You’ll *never* be an eco warrior. You’re just an eco worrier.’

‘Jumi, I...’

‘I don’t believe this. You’re just as bad as they are. I hate you. I never want to see you again!’ she shouted at him, attracting a few funny looks from passers-by.

‘Jumi!’ he called after her as she ran back towards the trouble.

‘Leave me alone!’ she shouted back over her shoulder. ‘You don’t care. If the planet dies it’s all your fault. You’re a waste of space. I’m going to find my dad.’

And with that she was gone.

How could she?

Marty trudged back home much more slowly than he'd left it. He should have been hurrying to try to be back before anyone realised he'd gone, but he really didn't care about that any more. Jumi hated him now, and he was back to having no friends again. How was he going to make any new friends ever again? Why hadn't he just told her who he was, right from the start?

He blamed himself for what had just happened. That entire riot was his fault. If only he'd messaged Jumi to warn her as soon as he found out about it. If only he hadn't lost his temper and had his phone and laptop taken away. She was right about him being a waste of space. He couldn't even tell his mum what he knew because he'd been scared he'd get into trouble. He felt terrible. It was an epic fail. The most epic of epic fails. Jumi was right, he was kidding himself if he thought he could ever be an eco warrior.

He entered Piccadilly Circus station and caught a tube train to Embankment, then walked from there slowly back to Westminster station. He found his lift, went back through the passage, and before long was back home.

He turned the TV on in his room. The news was on, of course covering the trouble at Oxford Street. “Riot Latest” was the headline on the screen, and they were showing footage of the windows getting smashed, the fighting and the confrontation with the police. It was weird to think he’d been there. The reporter was talking to the camera from the scene.

‘It’s all quiet here now,’ she said excitedly, ‘but that wasn’t the case an hour or so ago, when Eco Now protesters started causing damage to shops, terrifying members of the public and throwing missiles at the police.’

This was exactly how Skelton had planned it, with the protesters made to look bad. Missiles though? You could hardly call a few strawberry milkshakes *missiles*, could you?

‘A police spokesperson told us earlier,’ she continued ‘that a number of protesters had been arrested, including their notorious ringleader known as The Newt.’

Oh no! They’d arrested The Newt, and it was all Marty’s fault. Would The Newt go to prison, and if he did, how long for? Why hadn’t he just messaged Jumi before he lost his phone and laptop? He wondered what that would mean for Eco Now, and whether Jumi’s dad had got away without being injured or arrested.

‘The clean-up operation is now underway, but business owners told me earlier that they expect the cost of repairs to their buildings to run to millions of pounds.’

Millions? Unless it got a whole lot worse after Marty left there was no way that much damage had been caused. Skelton must have told them to say that.

The reporter had handed back to the newsreader in the studio now.

‘Well, joining me in our Westminster studio now is the Home Secretary Alan Fitch. Mr Fitch, we haven’t seen scenes like this on the streets of London for some time now.’

‘No we haven’t Melanie,’ said an uncomfortable-looking man whose voice Marty immediately recognised as Angry Alan. ‘This criminal activity is quite unacceptable. There’s a place for peaceful protest in this country, but Eco Now have today abused that right, and behaved in a manner that is completely intolerable. I’m sure they’ve done their own cause all kinds of damage today, as we can all see now that they’re nothing but a bunch of violent troublemakers.’

Alan was doing his job well, saying exactly the things that Skelton would have wanted to hear. He didn’t sound very angry now either, just a bit anxious.

‘They’re concerned about the proposed construction of Winston Churchill Airport I believe,’ said the newsreader. ‘Is it not the case that lots of people are actually worried about that?’

'But we can't allow these sorts of people to dictate Government policy. The new airport is vital for jobs, and will help to keep London and the United Kingdom at the forefront of the world economy. People need connectivity. It's crucial that it gets the green light.'

'So you're supporting the new airport then?'

'I am indeed Melanie. All this climate change nonsense is a load of old guff and the sooner we all accept that the better.'

'It's not a load of old guff, and you lot started the riot so you could lock up the protesters!' Marty shouted at the TV in frustration.

'Some people have been questioning though,' continued the interviewer, 'why there was such a large police presence at the rally today. Did you have information to suggest that there was going to be trouble?'

Marty wondered how Alan was going to answer that one, but he simply didn't.

'The point is Melanie, that today Eco Now have shown their true colours and it's clear that we shouldn't listen to a word they say.'

'But, Home Secretary, that doesn't answer my...'

'Now, if you'll excuse I have to be somewhere else,' Alan declared, and just walked off.

Well, Alan would certainly be in Skelton's good books after that performance. It made Marty even more miserable. How could anyone possibly stop Skelton and his super-rich friends now?

There was a knock on his door, which opened before he had time to answer. It was Emily.

‘Get out,’ he told her. ‘What’s the point of knocking if you just come straight in?’

She ignored him and went in anyway.

‘That’s no way to speak to someone who’s about to give you your phone back is it?’ she told him with a smirk. ‘Mum said you can have it now.’

She held it out towards him between her thumb and forefinger, just out of his reach.

‘Give it here,’ he told her, trying to grab it.

She jerked her arm away as he tried to grab it, before relenting and handing it to him.

‘Where’s my laptop?’ he demanded, checking his phone to see if there were any messages from Jumi. There were some from earlier, before the rally, asking where he was, but nothing after that. He immediately messaged her to ask if she was OK.

Emily picked up his laptop from the landing behind her, and he snatched it off her.

‘So, what have you been doing today?’ Emily asked him, sitting down on the edge of his bed. He thought about telling her get off, but didn’t think there was any point.

‘Not much,’ he lied.

She looked at him like she didn’t believe him. His phone chimed as a message came back. It was from Jumi, but it just told him to leave her alone.

‘Where’s Mum?’ he asked Emily.

‘In meetings.’

‘Of course she is. Don’t know why I even asked.’

‘Some emergency meeting I think she said. About those riots earlier.’

That got his attention.

‘Really?’ He realised he sounded a bit too interested. ‘I’ve just been watching that on the news.’

‘Terrible wasn’t it.’

‘Mm. Where is she, here or at the House of Commons?’

‘Here I think. Cabinet Office. Why?’

‘Oh, I was just wondering.’

‘Well, the meeting’s going on now, then she said she had some phonecalls to make. You might be able to see her after that if you need to.’

‘OK, thanks.’

She got up and left without another word.

Marty closed the door behind her and quickly got to work on his laptop. He logged in as quickly as he could and waited to hear what was being said in the meeting, hoping that it could be something useful, although what he’d do about it if it was he had no idea.

He couldn’t hear anything though. He checked to see that he’d logged in properly, and that all the settings were right, but he couldn’t find any problems. Maybe the meeting had finished. Maybe the battery in the pen-bug had died. He didn’t know how long it was meant to last.

Then he did hear something.

'Hello? Sir Jarvis?' It was Mum. It sounded like she was on the phone. Emily had said she was going to make some calls. Why was she ringing Skelton though? 'It's Charlotte... The riot? Yes, yes it was terrible wasn't it... You're absolutely right…'

There was a long pause, presumably as she listened to what the Chancellor had to say.

'I completely agree. We can't let it continue. There's absolutely no place for behaviour like that in our country.'

There was another long pause. Marty really wished he could hear the other side of the conversation.

'I can't say that I totally approve, but sometimes you have to make difficult decisions don't you… Yes… No, it wouldn't be at all good if they were all released. Do you think there's anything we can do to make sure that they're not?'

Another annoying pause.

'Well, we could do that of course. Do you know anyone with the skills to plant fake evidence at the protester's houses?... And what sort of evidence are we talking about here?... Weapons?... My word, that really would look bad for them wouldn't it. They'd be behind bars for years. By the time they got out the airport would be up and running… I agree, it's not ideal but it's the best we can do in the situation. Go ahead and make the necessary arrangements.'

That was it. He'd heard enough. How could she be saying those things? This was all so wrong, and now Mum was just as bad as the others. They were going to get innocent people locked up for things they hadn't done, including maybe Jumi's dad, and destroy Chumley Woods just so people could make money. He didn't care if she found out he'd been spying on her, he had to get her stop what she was doing. How could she have let herself get involved with this? He stormed out of his room, down the stairs and along the corridor to the Cabinet Office.

He flung the door open and barged into the room to confront his mum, but she wasn't there. Instead, smiling at him sweetly, was his sister.

We need a plan

He was speechless for a few seconds.

'You're not Mum,' he finally managed.

'Good spot.'

'Where is she?'

'Out.'

'But… she can't be out. I just heard her talking on the phone.'

'No, you didn't. You heard me.'

Marty suddenly remembered how alike Emily and Mum sounded. In one way it was a relief that Mum hadn't been saying those things, but what was actually going on?

'Well done for accidentally admitting you were listening in though,' Emily carried on. 'I was pretty sure you were.'

Whoops. He'd put his foot in it now.

'Listening device in your pen was it? I've got one of those too, remember? I guessed that must be why you kept leaving your pencil case in here. You clearly weren't doing any homework. You really should have left a folder with some actual work in it rather than just blank sheets of paper,' she said, leafing through his folder to illustrate her point before chucking it down on the table, just the way a teacher would. 'This is basic stuff Marty. You're just not devious enough to get away with something like this. You'll never be a politician.'

'I wouldn't want to be.'

'Plus you were going on yesterday about someone making a protest look like a riot. It was obvious you knew something.'

'It's true. That's what they did. They're dodgy as anything. You wouldn't believe some of the things I've heard them say.'

'You do realise how serious it is that you've been spying on them, don't you?'

He just glared at her. She was loving this.

'Are you going to tell Mum?'

'That depends.'

'On what?'

'On how much you tell me.'

He didn't like where this was going, but he could see he didn't really have a choice.

'What do you want to know?'

'Everything. I want to know why you, even though you hate politics and find it completely boring, are suddenly interested enough to spy on Cabinet meetings.'

He decided he may as well tell her. He couldn't think of a good reason not to. He took a deep breath.

'Well, I didn't actually mean to at first. I accidentally left my pencil case in here and wanted to know when they'd finished so I could get it back, and I heard them talking about this new airport. A friend of mine had sent me some stuff about it, so I was quite interested, and I listened in again, but this time I heard Skelton…'

'The Chancellor?'

'Yeah, him - looks like a vampire - threatening one of the other ministers, Alan he's called, before the meeting, making him support the airport.'

'Alan Fitch? What do you mean, threatening him?'

'He was going to get a story in the papers about his son getting caught stealing at school, saying that Alan forced the school not to expel him.'

'Blackmail?'

'Yeah. He tried to bribe him first, but that didn't work so he blackmailed him instead.'

'To support the airport?'

'Yeah. And now he does. Support it.'

'OK. Anything else?'

'Then I heard him arranging the riot yesterday.'

'What do you mean, "arranging the riot"?'

'He set it all up, Skelton. He said he'd got some people to pretend they were protesters but really they were there to cause trouble. And he'd made sure the riot police were there, and the TV cameras.'

'So, all those people who were arrested…'

'…Were completely innocent.'

'Marty, if this is all true…'

'It is. I promise.'

It was actually a relief to have told someone what he knew, whether she believed him or not.

‘Oh, and by the way,’ said Emily, ‘I saw you on the news, at the riot. You were in the background, just for a second, but it was definitely you. How did you get out of here when you were grounded?’

He didn’t want to tell her that, and he was relieved to hear the door starting to open, interrupting them. His relief didn’t last long though. The door remained ajar, and they heard an all-too-familiar voice in the corridor.

‘Barry, Alan, in here. Quickly.’

It was Skelton. Talk of the devil. Neither of them wanted to be caught by him just then. They frantically looked around for somewhere to hide. The Cabinet Office didn’t have much to offer in terms of hiding places, but it did have those long curtains. They weren’t drawn, but there was still just enough room behind them, and they were the only choice they had. They both raced over and hurled themselves behind them.

From their hiding place, keeping completely still and trying not to breathe too loudly, Marty and Emily heard Skelton again, now inside the room. Marty was convinced Skelton would hear them, and desperately tried to breathe quietly.

‘We’re nearly there,’ began Skelton. ‘Those Eco Now maggots have been taken care of and you’re doing exactly as you’re told now Alan. That just leaves Clive and our dear Prime Minister.’

‘Clive will never change his mind, will he?’ they heard Alan say. ‘He never changes his mind.’

'Oh, I think you'll find that Clive will cease to be a problem very shortly as soon as he finds out what I've got planned for him,' chuckled Skelton.

'What's that?' asked Barry.

'Put it this way. I wouldn't be at all surprised if he found himself in the headlines for all the wrong reasons very shortly. I predict an embarrassing and deeply personal scandal to be all over the news. He'll deny it of course but it'll be too late. Mud sticks, as they say. No smoke without fire. And of course, there'll be a number of witnesses to back up the allegations against him. He'll have no other option than to resign.'

'Why, what's he done?'

'He hasn't done anything you nincompoop,' snapped Skelton. 'We're just making it look like he has.'

'Ohhh… I get it,' said Barry slowly.

'Are you not even going to offer him the option to change his mind before the story goes live?' asked Alan, who was clearly a bit quicker on the uptake and had of course been through the same thing himself.

'No point. He's a bit weird but he's a man of principle. He wouldn't give in to blackmail or accept a bribe.'

'I'm not sure we should go straight in with… '

'Do you have a problem with what we're doing Barry? Would you like to find yourself implicated in a similarly embarrassing scandal? Just let me know if you want out?'

'No no no. I'm fine with… everything we're doing here.'

‘Good. I’m very pleased to hear that.’

‘So what happens now?’

‘That just leaves the Prime Minister. She’s still annoyingly influential, and she’s still not saying whether she’s going to support the airport or not.’

‘Is there anything we can do about her?’

‘Leave it to me. If she’s looking forward to a long stay here in Downing Street I think we’ll find she plays ball. Everything’s going according to plan. As a matter of fact the bulldozers are already on their way to Chumley Woods as we speak. There’s no point in hanging around waiting for the inevitable. They’ll be knocking down Eco Now’s precious trees before the end of the week.’

Skelton and Barry laughed loudly at this. Alan wasn’t laughing though. Even though he was going along with their plan didn’t mean he had to like it. As the laughter died down they heard the door open then close again. Marty dared a peek out from the curtains, and saw Emily doing the same. Thankfully the politicians had all gone, and they both left their hiding place.

'I can't believe it,' said Emily. 'What you told me sounded so ridiculous, but I did wonder if you were capable of making something like that up.'

Everyone seemed to doubt Marty's ability to make stuff up.

'There's no doubt about it now,' she carried on. 'Skelton's a two-faced snake. I don't know why Mum trusts him.'

'He must be the most evil politician in the world ever.'

'There is a fair bit of competition for that title, but he's certainly a contender.'

'Definitely the creepiest though.'

'Yeah, I think he's got that one in the bag.'

‘We’ve got to tell her. She’s got to stop those bulldozers before it’s too late. Now you’ve heard him as well she’ll believe us.’

‘I’m not sure,’ said Emily thoughtfully. ‘I think we need a plan.’

The plan, part 1

'Are you sure this is going to work?' Marty asked his sister the following day.

'No,' she answered.

'No?'

'No, I'm not *sure* it's going to work. I *think* it will though. Anyway, it's the best idea we managed to come up with isn't it?'

'Yeah, I guess. What if he sees through it though?'

'Have you got a better idea?'

'Well, no.'

'Right, so we've got to give this a try then haven't we?

'I suppose so.'

They'd wracked their brains until late into the night, trying to think of a way they could stop Skelton and his mates in their tracks, and what they were about to try was definitely the best they could come up with. It was the first time they'd agreed on anything in years. Marty wasn't sure it would be good enough though. Skelton was clever and devious, and if anyone was going to realise there was something fishy going on, it was him.

'Are you ready?' Emily asked him.

'Ready as I'm ever going to be.'

'And it's definitely going to record?'

'Definitely,' he confirmed, placing his pen-bug next to the phone. As long as the phone was on speaker it would pick up both sides of the conversation, and he had changed the settings on his laptop so that everything would be recorded.

They'd spent the morning preparing for what they were about to do. Even though she'd fooled Marty, Emily had watched some recordings on YouTube of Mum giving interviews to help her practice sounding even more like the Prime Minister, and he'd done his best to give her some guidance on how Mum spoke to Skelton from what he could remember from the meetings he'd listened to. Emily had casually asked Mum over breakfast what her plans for the day were, so they could be sure she was safely out of the way. Skelton wasn't going to believe it was Mum on the phone if she was sat next to him at the time. They'd also decided to use the phone in the Cabinet Office so that Skelton would recognise the number when he answered. There was nothing more they could do to prepare. All that was left to do was carry out their plan.

'OK, let's do this then,' Emily said.

She took a deep breath, and dialled.

Marty held his breath.

The phone rang once, twice, then was answered.

'Good morning,' said Skelton.

'Ah, Sir Jarvis, Charlotte here,' said Emily.

'Charlotte, how lovely to speak to you as always,' smarmed Skelton. 'And what can I do for you on this beautiful morning?'

It sounded like he believed he was talking to the Prime Minister. That was a good start.

'Sir Jarvis, I really wanted to catch up with you regarding this airport business.'

'Airport business, indeed.'

'I'm rather concerned about the damage that all these protests and criticism about climate change could be doing to us as a party.'

'I can assure you that I share your concern, Charlotte.'

'The longer this drags on, the more we look indecisive. We're suffering in the opinion polls as a result.'

'I quite agree.'

'So I've come to the decision that I as Prime Minister, and we as the Cabinet need to make a decision as to our stance in the debate. We can't just sit on the fence any longer.'

'Well, this is music to my ears indeed Charlotte. I've made my feelings on the matter very clear.'

'Yes you have Sir Jarvis.'

'So, what stance do you anticipate taking?'

'On balance I feel there's more to gain from building it than from not building it.'

'My thoughts exactly. Think of the jobs and the boost to the economy. We can't afford for the UK to fall behind the rest of the world because businessmen are unable to fly in and out of the country, can we now?'

So far, so good thought Marty.

'But, you seemed rather undecided last time we met,' continued Skelton. 'What's happened to change your mind?'

They knew he'd be cautious.

'I don't want to risk any more riots like the ones we've just had.'

'There's no guarantee that announcing a decision will stop further riots from occurring. Those protesters are vicious.'

'True, but there would be less for the protesters to gain,' said Emily. 'I think this will send a strong message to the country that this Government will not be intimidated by anybody.'

'I agree with you one hundred and ten percent Charlotte. We have to show the people who's in charge. It's the best for the party too. There's always an election around the corner.'

'I thought I would tell you first Sir Jarvis, as you are so well-respected in Cabinet. I've noticed how much influence you have over some of your colleagues.'

Marty's palms started to get sweaty. This was the crucial point that could make or break their plan.

'Really Charlotte?' replied Skelton warily. He was clever enough to know that he risked walking into a trap if he said too much. 'Well, that's very flattering, but I'm not sure I have any more influence than the next man.'

'Oh, but I think you do. I've noticed for example how Alan seems to follow your lead.'

This really rang alarm bells for him. Had he smelt a rat? The next few seconds were crucial. Skelton said nothing.

'It's quite alright Sir Jarvis. I know how these things work.'

'These things Charlotte? I'm not sure I quite follow,' said Skelton, trying to sound all innocent.

'I've had a quick chat with Alan. I know all about the consultancy role that was made available to him.'

'Ah, yes. I think he may have mentioned something to me about that too. He decided against it in the end I believe.'

'Come now Sir Jarvis. You've nothing to hide. I have no problem with it whatsoever. In fact, how can I put this? This is a little embarrassing, but actually, I was wondering whether you might be aware of any other businesses that might be on the look-out for a new consultant.'

'Oh?'

'You see, despite what some people might think, the role of Prime Minister doesn't actually pay particularly well.'

'I am aware of that.'

'And if someone became Prime Minister who, shall we say, might have a few debts from her past that she's struggling to pay off, on top of school fees etcetera, she might find that a second income would be extremely useful.'

'Ah, I think I know where you're coming from Charlotte.'

'I hoped you might say that Sir Jarvis.'

'Hmm. Well, it's funny you should mention it, because I do believe that a certain acquaintance of mine, one who happens to own a construction company based not too far from London, did mention to me at our club the other day that he might be looking to take on a new consultant. I'm sure he'd be willing to pay a considerable amount to the right candidate, if you see what I mean.'

'That's very interesting Sir Jarvis, very interesting indeed.'

'He would be delighted to hear you say that Charlotte. Absolutely delighted.'

'Do you think he might be interested in setting up a meeting Sir Jarvis?'

'I'm sure he would Charlotte. Would you like me to ask him?'

'I think I would Sir Jarvis. Thank you.'

'No, thank you Charlotte. I'll be in touch.'

'Thank you Sir Jarvis. I look forward to hearing from you.'

Emily ended the call, and they both let out a huge sigh of relief.

'It worked,' said Marty.

'Of course it did. I never had any doubts,' Emily told him. He didn't bother pointing out to her that she had.

'Now we just have to tell Mum what we've been doing and get her to agree to the second part of the plan.'

'Oh yeah,' said Emily with a frown. 'The easy bit…'

Telling mum

They had to wait a couple of hours for Mum to get back, and when she did she was then in meetings for another hour or so, but they finally managed to sit down with her around the kitchen table. Marty turned the TV off so no-one would be distracted. They'd agreed that Emily would do most of the talking, on the grounds that Mum was probably more likely to listen to her.

Mum took a sip from her water bottle. She already looked worn-out from a long day. Her children weren't about to help with that.

'OK. What's so urgent then?' she asked them expectantly.

'I'm not sure where to start,' said Emily.

'At the beginning?' Mum suggested.

'Right,' said Emily, and told her everything, from Marty accidentally hearing the first meeting, sneaking out to go to the rally, overhearing Skelton threatening Alan Fitch then boasting of the bribes he'd received and organising the riot, what Marty saw actually happen at the riot, Emily tricking him and then the two of them tricking Skelton.

Mum just listened as Emily talked, with Marty occasionally chipping in. After they'd finished she looked from Emily to Marty and back to Emily, trying to work out if they were telling the truth. Then she seemed to make up her mind.

'Very good, very good.'

'What?' said Marty.

'This is some sort of creative writing project is it? "What I did on my holidays" kind of thing, but made more exciting? It's actually really good. You two should think about writing a book.'

Finally, someone thought Marty was capable of making something up, albeit with some help from his sister, but just when he didn't want them to.

'No Mum,' explained Emily. 'We're not making it up, any of it.'

'OK, that's enough now,' she told them, starting to get up. 'You nearly had me going for a minute, but let's not keep the pretence going any more. I've got a million and one things to do and I haven't got time to…'

'No! Mum! Listen to us!' Marty shouted. This was going to turn into another row wasn't it? 'We're telling the truth, and we can prove it.'

That got her attention, and she sat back down.

'Proof? Proof of what exactly?'

'Proof that Skelton is ready to bribe you, the Prime Minister, to support him and his stupid airport,' he told her.

'Marty, can we just…'

'Listen to this,' he said, and hit play on his laptop.

'*Good morning,*' came the unmistakable voice of Skelton.

'*Ah, Sir Jarvis, Charlotte here,*' said what sounded like Mum.

'*Charlotte, how lovely to speak to you as always. And what can I do for you on this beautiful morning?*'

They had her attention now.

'Is that you Emily?' she asked, frowning.

Emily nodded.

Together they listened to the whole of the recording, as Skelton responded to being told about the Prime Minister's supposed financial problems by offering her a dodgy deal. Mum actually gasped when she heard him say '*I'm sure he'd be willing to pay a considerable amount to the right candidate, if you see what I mean.*'

Mum looked visibly shaken when the recording finished. Emily and Marty exchanged a nervous glance as they waited to see what she did next. He could see her thinking it all through.

Then she reached a decision.

'OK,' she began. 'First of all I have to say that what you've been doing, listening in on Cabinet meetings, was very, *very* wrong. We could have been talking about all sorts of matters of national security, discussing top secret information that could cause massive problems if it fell into the wrong hands. If it was anyone else doing it and they were found out they'd probably be jailed for a very long time.'

It sounded like she was going to punish Marty rather than trying to stop Skelton.

'I'm also very concerned that you managed to find out about the secret passage and leave the building without any sort of security and without anyone knowing where you were. Especially as you ended up in a riot.'

'It wasn't really a…' he started to say, but Mum silenced him with a look. This really wasn't going well.

'We'll talk about that later. However,' she carried on, 'I'll forget about all that for now because of what you've just told me, as long as you promise never to use the tunnel again.'

She looked at him expectantly, and he nodded reluctantly.

'I have had a few doubts about where the Chancellor's loyalties lay in the past, but I had no idea he was capable of this.'

'We can't let him get away with it.'

'You're right. It's disgusting what he's been doing, threatening people, taking bribes, offering bribes, getting innocent people locked up. It's all against the law. He's the one who should be locked up, not those protesters. The question is, how can we make sure that's exactly what happens?'

'We've got the recording that we just played you,' said Emily.

'Yes,' said Mum, 'but unfortunately he was careful enough to not actually offer me, I mean you, a bribe. He just hints at it. He could probably wriggle out of it if we accused him of anything, knowing how slippery he is, and it sounds terrible for me as well. Would everyone believe that I'd just been setting him up?'

'Well,' said Marty after a moment. 'That's where the second part of our plan comes in, but you've got to promise to make sure the airport doesn't go ahead.'

'Marty, I can't just make that sort of promise.'

'But Mum…'

'It's not just up to me. We have to wait for the vote in the House of Commons. It depends whether MPs give it the go ahead or not.'

'But what if it they want it to be built? Do you know how many species Chumley Woods is home to?'

'Well, I know it's quite a few…'

'It's more than a few,' he said, and he told her all he'd learned about Chumley Woods, loss of habitats, climate change and the sixth mass extinction.

'You're right Marty,' said Mum when he'd finished. 'That is something we should be concerned about. But just because the Chancellor has been breaking the law trying to get the airport built doesn't automatically mean that building it's the wrong thing to do. There are some genuine arguments for building it too. We have to balance them all up.'

'But Mum,' said Emily, 'just dealing with Skelton isn't enough. If the airport gets built, he's won. He'll still profit from it, and so will all his friends.'

'Talking of which,' Mum added, 'I'd love to know who else is involved in his little scheme – which businesses and journalists are in on it.'

'I don't think he'll ever tell you that,' said Emily.

'Which means they'll get away with it,' said Marty. 'The only way to make sure their plan doesn't work is to make sure the airport doesn't happen.'

Mum pursed her lips. He could see she wasn't happy with the thought of that happening.

'OK, I'll think about it,' she agreed.

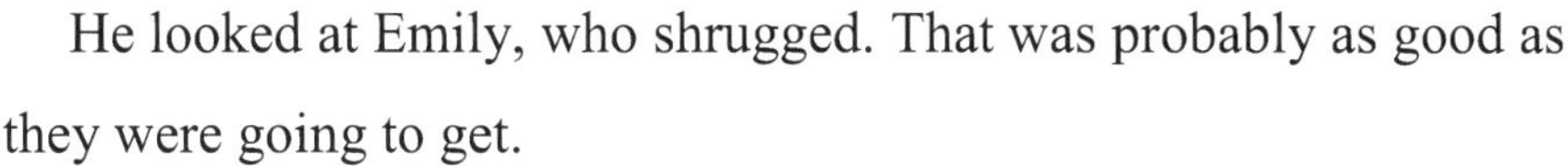

He looked at Emily, who shrugged. That was probably as good as they were going to get.

‘So,’ said Mum. ‘You’d better tell me the rest of your plan.’

The plan, part 2

'Ah, Sir Jarvis, come in, come in,' they heard Mum say.

Marty and Emily were listening in on the laptop in his bedroom as Mum tried to carry out the final part of their plan. He was also recording it, as they knew that they might need evidence of what was about to happen.

'Thank you for agreeing to see me at such short notice,' Mum said.

'My pleasure, Charlotte,' said Skelton.

The fact that he'd turned up was a good start. It didn't look like he'd smelt a rat yet.

'So, have you had a chance to look into my little proposition regarding consultancy work?'

'I have made a couple of enquiries, yes. Of course, I didn't let on who exactly I had in mind…'

'Of course.'

'… but, needless to say, my contacts were extremely interested in, how can one put it, securing the services of a high-ranking member of the Government.'

'That's encouraging news. And did your contacts have any particular figure in mind, that they might be willing to pay their new consultant for their services?'

'That would have to be agreed, but I think we can safely say that they wouldn't be overly worried by offering a six-figure sum, assuming that the services provided lived up to expectations of course.'

'Six figures! That's at least a hundred-thousand pounds,' said Emily, feeling the need to point out what Marty had easily worked out for himself (his maths was pretty good, even if no-one thought his creative writing was).

'Of course,' agreed Mum. 'And, what services exactly would they be looking for, from their "consultant"?'

'Well, let me put it this way. I believe they would be expecting to be able to take a flight from the newly-completed Winston Churchill Airport in the very near future.'

'Once all of the potential problems that could stand in its way, such as protesters, reasons for not building it that may or may not have been raised in Parliament and concerns about climate change have gone away?'

'Exactly Charlotte.'

'Well, I'm sure something can be arranged. After all, protesters do seem to have an unfortunate habit of finding themselves in prison, MPs can be convinced how best to vote and as for climate change - well, we all want to save the planet don't we, but if it means we lose out financially… maybe someone else can save the planet instead.'

'I can tell you're a lady after my own heart.'

'And we can always just claim that it's going to generate lots of jobs can't we, whether it is or not.'

‘Of course we can. That usually works.’

‘Right, well, I think we might have a deal then, Sir Jarvis.’

‘Excellent. I will let my associates know when I see them later.’

Marty looked at Emily with a frown. This was all going well, but had Skelton actually said enough to incriminate himself yet?

‘So,’ Mum continued. ‘When might I expect to receive the first of my payments as a consultant?’

Skelton gave one of his hideous, sneery laughs.

‘My dear Charlotte, not until after your services have been provided, of course.’

‘But, I’ve got school fees that need paying now.’

‘I’m ever so sorry, but that’s not quite how it works.’

‘What do you mean?’

‘Once work on the airport has started, then they’ll be able to pay you.’

‘Oh, right. So, if the airport doesn’t get built, I won’t get paid?’

‘Of course not. Why would they want to pay you if you haven’t fulfilled your part of the bargain? The airport gets built, or you don’t get paid.’

That was it! Surely that was enough now to prove that Skelton was offering a bribe to the Prime Minister to make sure that the new airport was approved. The two of them exchanged an excited glance.

‘Please tell me that’s still recording,’ Emily said.

Marty nodded. Mum seemed to think they’d got enough evidence now as well.

'So, Sir Jarvis. Am I allowed to know who your contacts are, now that I'm on board? I'd like to know who exactly I'm working with.'

'Ah, not quite yet Charlotte,' said Skelton. 'We'll get some details together, then perhaps we can arrange a meeting. All off the record, of course.'

'Of course. We wouldn't want anybody else to find out about this, would we... Or, would we?'

There was no sound for what sounded like an eternity. They waited to hear what would happen next. How would Skelton react to that?

'I beg your pardon, Charlotte,' he finally managed.

'I was just thinking Sir Jarvis, perhaps it would be a good idea for others to know what we've just been talking about. And about the conversation you had with Alan as well.'

'I'm not sure I quite understand what you're saying Charlotte,' said Skelton, sounding flustered. 'Why would we…'

'I think the whole world should know *exactly* what you and your little friends have been up to, don't you?' Mum told him, her voice getting louder and louder.

'Well, I…'

'Bribing a public official is a very serious crime, Sir Jarvis. How much did *you* stand to gain from the airport being built, eh?'

'Now look here, I'm not going to stand here and…'

'A six-figure sum at least, I'm sure. Or is it seven figures in your case?'

'I know,' Marty told Emily before she could say anything. 'That's millions.'

'Charlotte, I suggest you think about this before you do anything rash,' said Skelton, who sounded like he'd recovered a bit.

'And why's that?' Mum asked him.

'Well, for starters, you can't prove anything.'

'Oh, I can't prove anything can I?' she said. 'Take a look at what's on the end of the table.'

There was a pause.

'A pencil case?'

'Yes, a pencil case. A pencil case containing a rather special pen. A rather special pen that is also a listening device, which is at this very moment recording every word that we say, and has been for the last five minutes. So I can actually prove everything that you've just said.'

'Ah, but,' said Skelton, 'it's been recording everything *you've* said as well, so you sound just as bad as me. You can't let anyone hear it without implicating yourself as well.'

'Then it'll be your word against mine. Who do you think the public will believe Sir Jarvis?'

'Well, by the time it's been reported by all the newspapers and news channels that my family and friends own and run, I'm pretty sure most of the public will believe that I'm the innocent victim here, and that the Prime Minister has lost the plot, and is trying to set up one of her rivals to stop him from ever challenging her for the party leadership.'

'They'll never believe that.'

'Are you sure about that, Prime Minister?'

That wasn't good. That wasn't in the plan. They'd forgotten about his friends in the press. The press could make anything look like whatever they wanted to. Not all the papers and TV news channels would see it that way, but lots of them would. It would make Mum look terrible. It could ruin her career. What could they do now? What would Mum do now?

'I have witnesses though,' Mum told him, 'who knew that this was a set-up, and who have been listening in.'

'And who might they be?' asked Skelton, managing to sound bored of the whole thing.

'My children,' answered Mum.

Skelton let out another sneery laugh.

'Your *children*? Do you really think anyone's going to believe your own pathetic children? Oh, dear me. You're going to have to do a lot better than that. Now, if you'll excuse me, I have important business to attend to.'

It sounded like Skelton was gathering up his things to leave. Was that it? Had they failed?

'You're right,' said Mum. 'People probably wouldn't believe that my kids were doing anything other than just trying to stick up for their mum. What I could really do with is someone who you *wouldn't* expect would do anything to help me out as a witness. Someone who's been openly critical of me in the past perhaps. Someone with a reputation for trying to fight government corruption.'

'What are you talking about now Prime…'

'You can come out now,' Mum called in a loud voice.

Who was she talking to?

They heard Skelton gasp out loud.

'You're, you're…' he stammered.

'Most people call me The Newt,' said a man's voice that Marty recognised as, The Newt.

Another surprise

'How long have you been...'

'Behind the curtain? Oh, long enough, believe me. Long enough.'

'Oh look Chancellor,' Mum continued. 'I think what we have here is what you might call a witness. A witness who's been openly critical of me in the past. Someone with a reputation for trying to fight government corruption. Someone who was told beforehand what you were trying to do and who kindly agreed to hide behind the curtain to hear for himself. Just what I needed. How convenient.'

'But... but...'

'I think you'll find that that rather blows your little plan out of the water, don't you think?'

'But... but...'

'Come now, Chancellor, it's not like you to be lost for words. Maybe you'll have more to say to the police once they've arrested you. LEISHMAN!' she called.

Moments later they heard the door open.

'Yes Ma'am,' we heard Leishman say.

'Take the soon-to-be disgraced former Chancellor away and turn him over to the police would you. And advise them that they might want to try to find out exactly who his little chums helping him with this are as well.'

'Yes Ma'am,' Leishman repeated.

They heard the two of them leave the room, Skelton shouting and protesting as they went.

'This is outrageous! He should be in prison, not me! You can't do this to me! Don't you know who I am? I've got friends in high places you know! You won't hear the last of this! If you think this is over, then you are very much mistaken.'

Emily and Marty shared a high-five, then immediately felt more than a bit embarrassed.

'Did you know Mum was going to get The Newt to help?' Marty asked Emily.

'No,' she said. 'Good job she did though.'

'Yeah,' he agreed. 'Skelton might have got away with it if she hadn't.'

'Come on,' said Emily, and they both jumped up and ran downstairs to the Cabinet Office.

They flew through the doors and gave Mum a huge hug.

'We did it,' said Marty.

'We did,' Mum agreed. 'Thanks to you two and Mr Jones here.'

'Newt, please,' said The Newt. 'No-one calls me Mr Jones.'

Just then the door flew open again, and they all turned to see who it was. Marty half-expected it to be Skelton, having somehow given Leishman the slip, coming back to try to do more damage, but he was even more amazed when he saw who it actually was.

'Dad!' shouted Jumi as she ran in and gave The Newt a massive hug.

Dad?

'Is it all over?' she asked him. 'Did it work?'

'Yes it is, it did,' he told her.

Marty just stood there, literally with his mouth open.

'I believe you know this young lady,' said Mum.

He nodded.

'But I don't think you've met her dad, Mr... The Newt.'

'Pleased to meet you Marty,' said the Newt, stepping away from his daughter to shake his hand. 'I've heard a lot about you.'

'Um, pleased to meet you too,' Marty managed. 'You didn't tell me The Newt was your Dad,' he said to Jumi.

'You never asked,' she answered, which was true, although to be fair Marty wasn't likely to have gone – "Is that random man over there your Dad?"

'I thought you'd been arrested though,' said Emily to The Newt.

'I was,' said The Newt, 'but your mum got in touch, told me what you'd found out was going on, and asked me if I wanted to help her put a stop to it. Of course, I said yes.'

'All of the other real protesters have been released as well,' added Mum, which was good. 'The police are tracking down the thugs who actually caused the damage.'

'So what happened?' asked Jumi. 'I couldn't hear anything from next door. It was terrible, just sitting there, wondering if it was going to work. I did hear that creepy guy shouting on his way out though, so I guessed it went OK.'

'He fell for it completely,' said Emily.

'It was just as well your dad was here to witness it though,' said Mum.

'So does this mean the airport isn't going to be built then?' asked Jumi.

'Not quite,' said Mum. 'Sir Jarvis won't be able to do any more to bully it through, but we've still got to vote on it in Parliament.'

'But surely you can't build it now,' Marty told her.

'We've got to win the vote tomorrow,' said Mum. 'I haven't got the power to make the decision on my own, but I will be doing everything I can to persuade my fellow MPs not to vote for it.'

'That's good to hear,' said The Newt.

'But why can't you just call off the vote?' Marty asked.

'I promised we'd look at building a new airport when we won the election,' Mum told him. 'If I just abandon the idea that will give it will look like we lied to the country to get elected.'

'Wouldn't be the first time that's happened,' scoffed The Newt, before adding 'Sorry. Force of habit.'

'If people lose their trust in us and vote us out who knows what the next government would think about the environment.'

'I guess,' Marty reluctantly agreed. He'd still rather they scrapped the idea altogether, but he kind of saw her point.

'It's not going to be easy though,' she warned. 'I have a feeling that what you heard, Marty, might just have been the tip of the iceberg.'

'What do you mean?' he asked.

'I suspect they might have been busy bribing or blackmailing MPs for a while now. Plus there are quite a few who genuinely think building the airport is the right thing to do. The damage might already be done, and they might have secured enough votes to get it through. Just because Sir Jarvis is out of the picture doesn't mean this is all done and dusted.'

'There must be something you can do about it though?'

'Not really, unless anyone is brave enough to admit what's been happening. If they've taken a bribe they won't want to get caught, and if they're being blackmailed they may still be too scared to say anything. It might be too late already. I'll call a Cabinet meeting before the vote tomorrow so I can try to deal with them, but I don't know how they'll react. I might not be able to change their minds.'

Marty sighed. They'd all been so excited about getting rid of Skelton. Now they were all standing round looking miserable.

'So, what happens now then?' asked Jumi.

'Well,' answered Mum, 'before we do anything else I think we all need to eat. I thought you two could stay for dinner, if you'd like to of course.'

She caught sight of the nervous looks on her children's faces.

'Don't worry. I'll ask Chef to cook us something as we've got guests. I'm not going to cook myself. It wouldn't look good if the Prime Minister rescued the country's leading environmental protester from prison then brought him back to Downing Street to poison him, would it?'

They all laughed.

'I'll go and speak to Chef now. Then I'd like to pick your brain about a few things if I may,' she told The Newt.

'That's fine,' he said, and she led him from the room.

Emily followed them, leaving Marty and Jumi alone.

'So you really are the Prime Minister's son then,' she said.

'Yeah.'

'And you really live in 10 Downing Street.'

'Yeah. Do you want the guided tour?'

'OK.'

Suddenly it did seem just a little bit cool to live in one of the most famous houses in the country. He was just glad to have his friend back though.

Before they could start the tour, Larry sidled his way into the room. He made a bee-line for Jumi and started to rub his head against her legs.

'He likes you,' Marty said. 'This is…'

'Larry,' said Jumi. 'I know. He's famous.'

She sat down and started to stroke the Chief Mouser. Marty sat down next to them.

'I'm sorry,' he told her.

'About what?'

'Sorry I never told you who my mum was.'

'That's OK. I never told you who my dad was either.'

'No more secrets?'

'No more secrets.'

They both smiled.

'And I'm sorry I was more worried about getting into trouble, or my Mum losing her job, than stopping the airport,' he added.

'It's fine. You got there in the end.'

Marty watched her playing with Larry for a while. He was quite selective with who he played with. He'd obviously found a friend there. He climbed onto her crossed legs and made himself comfortable.

'Does that mean though,' Marty said tentatively after a while, 'if your Dad's The Newt…'

'No, don't say it…'

'That your nickname's Tadpole?'

She glared at him, then smiled.

'I do usually punch anyone who calls me that, but I can't exactly move at the moment.'

'Larry to the rescue again then,' he grinned.

'Why, when has he come to the rescue before?' she asked.

'Oh, it's a long story. I'll tell you some time.'

'OK. Well, anyway. If you call me Tadpole, I'll call you Marty Farty.'

'No way.'

'So do we have a deal then?'

'Yeah, I guess we do. There was a Prime Minister once called Tadpole though.'

'What?'

'Possibly, anyway.'

This was good. He was starting to feel happy, for the first time since he'd moved in, sat there with Jumi and Larry. He couldn't relax yet though. Skelton might have been caught out, but they hadn't won yet. How much damage had he already done? Had he already secured the votes he needed to push the airport through?

Marty thought about the woods. About the foxes, badgers, hedgehogs and birds. About the Newt and the others who'd been locked up for no good reason. About Skelton, and the bribes and the threats. And he knew. He knew someone was going to have to do something about it. And that someone was going to have to be him.

He'd failed by not telling anyone what he knew straight away, and when he hadn't warned Jumi about the riot, and without Emily's help they probably wouldn't have caught Skelton. This time it was down to him. He wasn't going to let Jumi down again. He had to think of a way to stop some of the MPs who'd been bullied by Skelton voting for the airport.

He thought about it and thought about it, and eventually, he came up with a plan.

Crunch time

If you'd told Marty he'd be getting up at 7.30am during the school holidays he'd have told you you were crazy, but that's what time he'd set the alarm on his phone for (set to vibrate so no-one else would hear it). He had work to do. He quickly got dressed and sneaked out of the secret passage before anyone else was up. Well, his mum was probably up but she wasn't around, which was good as he'd promised her he wouldn't use the passage any more. Luckily, he'd had his fingers crossed behind his back, although he still wasn't entirely sure why that made any difference.

As he headed for the station exit he passed a news kiosk and glanced at the newspaper headlines. There was no mention of Skelton's arrest yet, but most of them seemed to be saying that MPs should vote for the airport. Skelton's friends were clearly still following the plan. Would that mean that the MPs they'd already got on board would do the same? There didn't seem to be anything scandalous about Clive in the papers though, like Skelton had said there would be, although they still might have found a way to get even him to vote for the airport.

Marty left the station and headed for the nearest shops he could find. He found the one he wanted, a pharmacy, and bought a couple of packs of what he was after. Then he walked on until he found a supermarket and bought some more there, not wanting to buy them all in the same place as it might look a bit suspicious. He thought he probably had enough then, so he ran back to the station and home.

When he got back, he headed straight for the Cabinet Office, desperately hoping he'd get there before the big pre-debate meeting started. His mum had told them she was going to tell the other ministers about Skelton, but she wasn't hopeful any of them would change the way they were going to vote. They had too much to gain or to lose.

He opened the Cabinet Office door and was relieved to see find the room empty. First, he opened the curtains and let the hot morning sunshine straight into the room. He felt the heat pouring in straight away. Hopefully the room would soon be like a sauna. Then he turned his attention to the big jugs of water that were already in position on the table. He did what he needed to do and quickly retreated from the room.

* * *

'Hurry up, it's starting,' called Jumi.

Marty did hurry up, back to his seat in front of the TV. She'd come round to watch Parliament debate the new airport with him and Emily. For once Marty was happy to watch politics on the telly. Just this once.

The House of Commons was packed today. Everyone had turned up to listen and vote. There weren't even enough seats for everyone, and some of the MPs had to stand. Marty thought it was very bad planning to have more MPs than there were seats.

'The Prime Minister,' announced a woman in a black gown sitting right in the middle of the room.

'That's the Speaker,' Emily told the others. 'She's in charge of the debate.'

Mum got up to speak. She starting talking about everything she'd seen in the videos Jumi had sent Marty, which he'd made sure she watched too, about deforestation, carbon emissions and ocean pollution. She talked about big business and governments, about environmental protesters and species extinction. She was brilliant, and everyone seemed to listening to her every word. Everyone who was there at least.

'I can't see Skelton,' said Emily.

'Maybe he's watching from his prison cell,' suggested Jumi.

Marty said nothing. He was closely watching the seats either side of where Mum had been sat, where the rest of the Cabinet were sitting. Were one of two of them looking a bit uncomfortable, or was he imagining it?

Mum was still speaking. Now she was talking about the arguments that others had given for building the airport, and for a second Marty was worried that she'd changed her mind, before she promptly told the MPs why they should ignore those arguments.

Then it started to happen. A bald-headed man a couple of seats down from Mum suddenly jumped up as if he'd been stung by a wasp and hurried out, attracting no more than couple of puzzled glances from the MPs around him. That was Bald Barry gone. Was Marty's plan working, or was it just a coincidence? He looked at the other Ministers. Some of them were definitely shuffling around and looking a little anxious. Was that just because of what was at stake, or was it something else?

Just then, Jumi had a text.

'It's my Dad,' she said. 'He's with some of the Eco Now guys at Chumley Woods. He says the bulldozers are out in force, but they seem to be waiting for the go-ahead from somebody.'

'Let's hope it never comes,' said Emily.

Marty nodded, but he was still focused on the screen, and it happened a second time. The lady next to Mum, who he had noticed had switched from wiping her nose with a hankie to mopping her brow with it, grabbed her handbag and ran to the exit. That must have been Hayfever Henrietta. This time a few more people noticed.

Seconds later a lady wearing thick glasses followed them both – Glasses Gurinda. Marty risked a grin. His early morning trip to the shops looked like it was going to pay off. He really hoped there was a toilet nearby.

When a man Marty now recognised as the Home Secretary, Angry Alan Fitch, became the fourth Cabinet Minister to suddenly rush out people really started to notice. There was a buzz in the debating chamber, and the presenter on the TV wondered what was happening.

'Where are they all going?' asked Emily. 'What's going on?'

'Dunno,' Marty lied.

'They're going to miss the vote.'

'Oh yeah, that's a shame isn't it,' he said innocently, and got a quizzical look back.

Mum carried on as if nothing was happening though, even when a man who looked like that teacher that every school has who tries much too hard to be trendy, who could only have been Cool Clive, made it five Ministers vacating their seats.

'I've never seen anything like this,' said Emily. 'Marty, what have you done?'

'Me? Why do you think it's going something to do with me?'

Emily looked at him with a highly suspicious look on her face. He pretended not to notice.

After a couple more minutes Mum brought her speech to an end, saying, 'I will be voting against the destruction of Chumley Woods, and against the building of the new airport, and I ask you all to do the same.'

She sat down to a loud chorus of MPs shouting 'hear, hear, hear!', which Emily explained is what they do when they like what someone has just said.

'That seemed to go well then,' said Marty.

'Yes it did,' said Emily, 'but it's going to be close, even without Skelton and if Fitch and the others don't make it back in time. You never really know until they've voted on it.'

'Is that what happens now?' asked Jumi.

'Yeah,' answered Emily. 'They go off into one room if they agree with Mum that it shouldn't be built, or into another if they think it should, and someone counts how many people are in each one. The room with the most people in it wins.'

'Could they not just press a button or something?' Marty asked.

'You'd think so, wouldn't you? Anyway, it takes a while, so we've just got to wait. Not everyone looked like they agreed with her, so it might be close. It all depends on how many people have been nobbled.'

'Nobbled?'

'Nobbled. Bribed or bullied.'

'Sounds painful,' he joked, but nobody was in the mood to laugh. This was it. It was crunch time.

They waited in silence for what seemed like forever. Marty's stomach was in knots. He felt terrified but excited at the same time. On the TV the presenters burbled away about very little, filling time, just waiting for something to happen. First they spoke to one expert who thought the result would go one way, then to another who thought exactly the opposite.

Marty needed the toilet, not as urgently as some of the MPs had just now, but he still needed to go. He didn't want to miss anything whilst he was gone though. It was probably just nerves anyway. His heart was pounding. Jumi also looked really nervous. Emily checked her phone for updates, but whatever they were she kept them to herself. He looked at his watch, but he didn't know when they'd started voting, or how long it would take so that told him nothing. Jumi got another message from her dad. The bulldozers were still being held at bay.

On the TV the MPs were starting to return to their seats, slowly filling up the green padded benches. After a while all the seats had been filled, and it was standing room only again. Marty wondered whether anyone who'd been standing at the start had nicked a seat off someone who been lucky enough to have one for the debate. The seats next to Mum were occupied again now, but not by their original occupants. Hopefully that meant they hadn't managed to get into a voting room either.

Marty really needed the toilet now, but he was convinced that it would all start happening the second he left the room. He considered pretending to leave the room, then coming back, to see if that had the same effect, but he decided that would just be stupid.

Eventually, two men and two women made their way through the crowd towards the Speaker, clutching sheets of paper.

'This is it, this is it,' said Emily excitedly. 'They've got the result.'

The Eco Warrior

The men and women handed their pieces of paper to the woman Emily said was called The Speaker. She looked at them carefully, then cleared her throat.

‘The ayes to the right – 312 votes,’ she announced grandly. ‘The noes to the left – 313 votes. The noes have it, the noes have it!’

‘Yes!’ shouted Emily, giving a little fist-pump.

A great cheer went up from the MPs, and the camera panned back to Mum, who looked very pleased and was being congratulated by the people now sitting next to her. It looked good, but Marty had no idea what ‘ayes’ and ‘noes’ were.

‘Did we win?’ he asked.

‘Yes, we won,’ said Emily with a huge grin. ‘By one vote!’

‘So the airport isn’t going to be built?’

‘No, it isn’t.’

‘Yes!’ he shouted at the same time as Jumi.

Marty and Jumi high fived, then she gave him a huge hug, and he was so excited he wasn’t even embarrassed.

'Thank you,' she told him. 'Thank you both, and your mum.'

'Jumi,' he said, 'I wouldn't even have known about Winston Churchill Airport or Chumley Woods if it wasn't for you, and we couldn't have beaten Skelton without your dad's help.'

'I suppose,' she accepted.

'And there's still lot's more to do,' he added.

'Talking of which,' said Emily, 'Mum's about to speak again. You might want to hear what she has to say.'

Mum got to her feet, then waited for the noise to die down.

'Today we haven't just made a decision not to build an airport. We've made a decision to put the planet first. For too long we've been making decisions, right here, that put making money before everything else. From now on, our planet has to come first. This is just one decision, one airport, one area of woodland saved, but, slowly and surely, we can keep making those decisions, and we can keep making a difference.'

Jumi's phone chimed.

'It's Dad. He says the bulldozers are leaving! The woods are safe!'

'We are just one country,' Mum continued on the TV. 'We need to persuade our friends all around the world to do the same. We've a long way to go, but I promise to do everything I can to persuade other world leaders to join us in our mission. This is something we simply have to do. We cannot afford to fail.'

She sat down to another round of 'hear, hears'.

'Hey Marty,' smiled Jumi. 'I don't know what you did, but it worked. Maybe you are an eco warrior after all.'

* * *

Later that evening, after Jumi had gone home, Marty sat down to eat a takeaway pizza with Mum and Emily. Mum had had a word with Leishman to make sure the delivery driver would be allowed through the security at the end of the street. The TV was off, and they just had some music playing quietly in the background.

‘That was very strange today, didn’t you think?’ said Mum in between mouthfuls.

‘What was?’ Marty tried to ask innocently.

‘All my Cabinet having to rush off to the toilet in the middle of a debate. They all suddenly came down with diahorrea apparently.’

‘Wow,’ he managed, carefully avoiding eye contact. He could feel Mum and Emily both watching him carefully though.

‘You wouldn’t know anything about it, would you?’

‘Me?’

‘Yes, you. I just wondered whether it might have anything to do with all those empty boxes of laxatives I found in the bin when I got home.’

Whoops. He really should have found a better place to get rid of those.

‘Marty! You didn’t?’ gasped Emily, sounding shocked, although she actually looked quite impressed.

‘Well, I…’ he began, but Mum interrupted him.

‘Best you don’t answer that. It’s just as well I always drink out of my own water bottle and never from the jugs of water on the table in the Cabinet Office though, I think, isn’t it? Especially with there being just one vote in it… A couple of them did say the water tasted a little funny, but someone had opened all the curtains and it was so hot in there that they drank it anyway.’

He helped himself to some more garlic bread, and kept his head down. Fortunately, Mum didn’t seem to want to know any more about it.

'So, what do have planned for the rest of the holidays then Marty?' Mum asked him after a while, in a blatant attempt to change the subject. 'Other than whatever homework it was you were supposed to be doing in the Cabinet Office that is,' she added.

'Well, I said I'd go skateboarding with Jumi tomorrow.'

'Right, well I'd better get Leishman to arrange some security for you.'

'It's fine. I can just use the secret passage again.'

'Which you *still* haven't told me how you get to,' moaned Emily.

'And he's not going to either,' Mum told them both with a stern look. 'Neither of you will be sneaking out of the secret passage any more. I might have just stopped an airport being built, but I'm not about to turn into some sort of new-age, free-spirited, Eco Now supporting earth-mother who lets her children come and go as they please.'

'What's wrong with Eco Now supporters?' Marty asked her. 'I thought you liked The Newt.'

'I did, I mean I do. In fact, I'm thinking of seeing if he's free to have dinner with me some time.'

'Don't tell me you're cooking for him,' Emily gasped.

'No,' said Mum, looking offended. 'I thought we could find a nice restaurant somewhere nearby.'

'Somewhere vegan of course,' said Marty.

'Oh, yes, of course,' said Mum, who clearly hadn't thought about the fact that the country's leading protector of animals might not eat meat.

'And you'll have to either walk or use public transport,' added Emily.

'Yes, I can do that,' Mum insisted.

'Are all your security guards going to squeeze onto the tube with you?' he asked. 'Leishman will love that.'

'I thought I saw something between the two of you,' said Emily.

'I don't know what you mean,' said Mum, blushing. 'I just think we have a lot to discuss.'

'You and the Newt could double-date with Marty and Jumi.'

Now it was Marty's turn to blush.

'Alright, alright' said Mum. 'That's quite enough of that thank you very much.'

They both got the message that it was conversation over. Marty wasn't at all sorry about that. They ate in silence for a while.

'I was also thinking I should spend more time with you two. I know I haven't had a lot of time for you since we moved in here. I need to do something about that. I'm going to make sure that changes.'

'OK,' said Marty, and Emily nodded.

'Starting from tomorrow,' Mum continued. 'I thought I could cook something nice for us all.'

He looked at Emily.

'Would now be a good time to tell you how to use the secret passage?'

Before you go

As Shakespeare once said, "Don't forget to rate and review Ian Slatter's book on Amazon!" *

I would be ***massively*** grateful if you could take a minute to rate/review my book. It really is quick and you don't have to write very much if you don't want to. Ratings and reviews are hugely important for indie authors like me. They can make the difference between readers choosing to read a book or not.

Thank you!

* It is possible that he didn't actually say that – a politician told me he did. **

** That may also not be true.

Free download offer

Read about Marty's next big adventure in this **free short story**:

Join my Readers Club and receive this **free short story**, plus updates about new books (including sneak peeks) and special offers.

Visit ianslatter.com for further details.

Printed in Great Britain
by Amazon

50370316R00104